Longarm shifted the saddle to his other hip as he moved along the hallway. He could see the waxed white stem of the match he'd left lodged in his door hinge long before he got there.

He lowered the saddle silently to the hall runner a good five paces short and quietly drew his six-gun as he moved in on the balls of his booted feet.

Covering the door with the revolver in his right hand, Longarm put his tingling left hand to the cold brass knob and when nothing happened he began to gingerly twist the same. The well-oiled latch moved silently, Lord love it, as it proved to be unlocked.

All Longarm knew, when first he flung the door open and chased his gun muzzle inside, fast and low, was that someone was just inside the door, outlined darkly by the brighter window light from behind. So the two of them went reeling across the rug to crash down together across the bed as Longarm hung on with one hand and raised the heavy six-gun with the other . . .

TABOR EVANS

LONGARM

AND THE GREAT MILK-TRAIN ROBBERY

JOVE BOOKS, NEW YORK

LONGARM AND THE GREAT MILK-TRAIN ROBBERY

A Jove Book / published by arrangement with the author

PRINTING HISTORY
Jove edition / March 2004

Copyright © 2004 by Penguin Group (USA) Inc.

ISBN: 0-515-13698-0

A JOVE BOOK®
Jove Books are published by The Berkley Publishing Group, a division of Penguin Group (USA) Inc., 375 Hudson Street, New York, New York 10014.
JOVE and the "J" design are trademarks belonging to Penguin Group (USA) Inc.

PRINTED IN THE UNITED STATES OF AMERICA

10 9 8 7 6 5 4 3 2 1

Chapter 1

Longarm, as Deputy U.S. Marshal Custis Long was better known around the Denver Federal Building and nearby Parthenon Saloon, was as bemused as other readers of the *Rocky Mountain News* by the desperados who'd stopped the Trinidad Milk Train not once, not twice, but three times in as many weeks, two hundred miles to the south. For the greater puzzle was not so much who they might be as why in thunder they'd *done* it!

The Reno Brothers, who'd invented train robbing back in the '60s, had ridden off with $96,000 after stopping the Jefferson–Missouri–Indianapolis in '68.

The more recent and more murderous James-Younger gang had averaged between the $75,000 taken from the Missouri–Pacific to the mere $2,000 that had cost the life of Engineer John Rafferty when they'd derailed his Iowa express near Adair.

But the four-man gang who'd robbed a *milk train* more than once . . . ?

All three trains they'd stopped in the wee small hours had of course been hauling early morning milk to the fewer than ten thousand inhabitants of Trinidad, nestled in the foothills where Raton Creek joined the slightly bigger Purgatoire River to bust loose from the Sangre de

Cristo Mountains and wind out across the Southern Colorado Plains.

Most every town of any size across the east or west was served much the same way by other early-morning short-haul local combinations. Dairy cows were milked around three in the afternoon and three in the morning and milk spoiled when kept much more than a day. So dairy farmers close enough to market hauled their produce to town themselves whilst those more than a three-hour haul behind their own teams took it to one of the milk stops located around six miles apart along the rail line to load it aboard their aptly named milk train. Since early risers along the line often had beeswax in the nearby town, the Trinidad Milk Train, like many others, had a freight car and passenger coach up ahead of the four milk cars. But the four-man gang hadn't searched the one freight car for valuables nor molested any passengers. They'd stopped the same milk train along different stretches of the AT&SFRR right-of-way they were using during off-hours of the cross-country traffic by blocking the tracks with a bluff of piled tumbleweeds on one occasion, a freight wagon parked on the tracks on another and, the last time, a roaring bonfire that had actually caused some damage to the roadbed.

But after stopping the train and ordering passengers and crew off at gunpoint, the four masked riders on nondescript horseflesh had wheeled their mounts to ride away, with one of them sounding that distinctive but hard to describe taunting laugh of the border buscadero or liquored-up vaquero. That didn't mean much, as the *Rocky Mountain News* pointed out and Longarm agreed. Any old boy could laugh like that if he put his mind to it, and by the tricky light of the crime scenes, if that was what one wanted to call them, their victims had been left with the impression they were Anglo riders, likely trying to shift the blame for whatever they thought they were doing to the fair-sized Mex community down Trinidad way.

2

Knowing the federal courts he rode for had no juris-diction in petty local foolishness, Longarm was inspired by the sheer stupidity as it read in the *Rocky Mountain News* to stop at an out-of-town newsstand on his own time to pick up an edition of Trinidad's *Chronicle News* in the hopes of a more lucid account of that last robbery.

He'd hoped in vain, he saw, as he read the local paper's more detailed but no more sensible coverage of what ap-peared no more than a dangerous Halloween prank carried out by grown men with real guns near the end of May.

After stopping Trinidad's morning milk just before dawn with that bonfire on the tracks, the whatevers, de-scribed by witnesses as full-grown men dressed as cow-hands with matching red print bandanas masking everything below their eyes, had forced everyone off the train, laughed like hell, and ridden off to the west along an old game trail leading nowhere's much in the rugged Sangre de Cristos. They couldn't have gotten far before their unharmed victims piled back aboard the milk train to pull the bonfire off the tracks with the engine's cow-catcher, streak past other milk stops to raise the alarm in the county seat of Trinidad, and unload to make room on board for the resultant sheriff's posse, horses and all.

The posse had detrained near the still-glowing embers at trackside to tear-ass west as the sun came up behind them. An early morning wagoneer they met a ways up the trail said four riders had indeed been going the other way, at a full gallop, farther up the trail about an hour back. The lawmen had galloped on and on, until they ran out of trail to gallop as they found themselves in a box canyon. The Sangre de Cristos were inclined to be like that.

Sangre de Cristo meant "Blood of Christ" in Spanish and Anglo folk who'd come along later felt no call to argue the description when they gazed up at the red sand-stone crags rising bare as the backbone of some dragon at any time of day and gleaming like fresh-spilled blood when the sunlight was hitting them at dawn from the east or sunset from the west.

A geologist Longarm drank with had told him the Sangre de Cristos to the south were the red sandstone hogbacks of the more northerly Front Range writ large. The so-called Garden of the Gods west of Denver was a much smaller version of the towering Sangre de Cristos.

Longarm didn't care. He knew they weren't about to send him two hundred miles into the field to round up milk train robbers who obviously didn't know what in blue blazes they were doing.

Longarm was hampered by his common sense. The mastermind behind the apparently pointless milk train robberies had known, or thought he'd known, exactly what he was doing.

Like Longarm, far to the north, the mastermind had felt safe in assuming he was setting up the sheriff of Las Animas County or at worse the Colorado State Troopers. But he'd had no way of knowing Governor Fred Pitkin drank with Federal Marshal Billy Vail of the Denver District Court, a lawman of the old school who read the fine print sharper than some of the congressmen who wrote the fool federal laws and, what the hell, old Fred was a good old boy and what were friends for?

By the Monday after the last early-morning robbery Longarm had more important matters than the tomfoolery down Trinidad way. Miss Morgana Floyd, the head matron of that Arvada Orphan Asylum, had come by two free tickets to the revival of *Fra Diavalo* at the opera house and said she was not about to attend the opening and sit up front in the orchestra row with another damn girlfriend.

When Longarm protested he'd seen the fool opera the last time it had ridden through Colorado and hadn't thought much of a singing contest betwixt outlaws resulting in only two deaths after all that fussing, Morgana Floyd allowed she'd be mighty disappointed in a beau who refused to sit through a grand opera with a lady just because he'd seen it before.

That was how gals told a man he wouldn't be getting any for a spell.

They told him they'd be disappointed in him.

The lackluster death toll of *Fra Diavalo* was not the problem. A private box overlooking the orchestra row from on high was the problem. It was hired every opera season by a certain brown-haired society gal who was likely to be disappointed indeed to see him seated with a petite brunette gal after telling her he couldn't make that opening with *her* because of night duty at the Federal House of Detention for the foreseeable future, or at least until the blamed opera left town.

Knowing nothing about his senior deputy's tangled love life, Marshal Billy Vail of the Denver District Court was braced for some argument as he sat at his cluttered desk that morning, enveloped in an octopus cloud of expensive but mighty pungent cigar smoke.

As the younger, taller, and leaner Longarm entered the oak-paneled inner office Billy Vail ran his eyes all over him for an excuse to cuss him out. But that morning Longarm had properly knotted the shoe-string tie that went with the store-bought tobacco tweed suit and vest he was required to wear around the federal building by the Reform Administration of fair but fussy President Hayes.

A deputy marshal on duty was *supposed* to be armed and so if anybody didn't cotton to the double-action Colt .40-44 worn cross-draw under the frock coat and peeking out with its tailored grips, they were free to write their congressman. Longarm's back-up double Derringer was concealed as all get-out at one end of the gold washed watch chain across his tweed vest. Longarm was allowed to conceal his badge and deputy's warrant until it came time to flash either. Ergo the only possible infraction betwixt the brim of his coffee brown Stetson and the soles of his stovepipe army boots was that three-for-a-nickel cheroot gripped in his teeth as he sat down uninvited across from his boss and flicked ash from the same on the office rug.

Vail shot a thoughtful glance at the banjo clock on one wall. Longarm wasn't late enough to matter that Monday morn. So Vail growled, "Watch where you flick them fucking ashes, dammit! Were you brung up in a barn?"

To which Longarm replied with a clear conscience, "Not hardly. But back in West-by-God-Virginia my poor but civilized parents provided ash trays for their visitors. What sort of shit detail might you have in mind for me this morning, boss?"

Vail blustered, "Who told you we were taking on that foolishness in Las Animas County? I'll have their gizzards on a plate!"

Longarm laughed and said, "I showed up early with this fool tie tied right so's you'd have no fair reason to fuss at me. So when you fussed at me anyhow . . . Did you just say Las Animas County, where they've had all those great milk train robberies?"

Vail grumbled, "I did. It's an election year and Fred Pitkin wants his own party man, an Anglo in good with the mining interests down yonder, to win the coming election against an infernal Eye-talian who's larnt enough Spanish to drum up support in the Corazon de Trinidad precinct. All this bullshit with the morning milk train has the sheriff in power feeling as foolish as he looks. So Fred and me figured, you being better than average at pointless bullshit . . ."

"There's always a point and how do we justify federal jurisdiction in what would seem on the surface an outbreak of local malicious mischief?"

"Interstate Commerce. Interfering with the same," Vail replied with an impish Halloween Night expression.

He went on to explain, "You raise beef cows on the lower range to the east of the Sangre de Cristo foothills and you graze smaller herds of dairy cows in the cooler

6

and greener mountain meadows of the foothills running north and south to the west of all the towns along the aprons of the Front Ranges. So that milk train they've taken to stopping at gunpoint three weekends in a row forms up for its morning run on the rail sidings at Maxwell, New Mexico Territory, forty-five miles to the south of Trinidad, Colorado. Are you with me so far?"

Longarm nodded soberly and said, "I am. That predawn milk train stops to take on milk cans every few miles and in the process steams through Raton Pass and across a state line which *we*, but neither the sheriffs of Las Animas County, Colorado, nor Colfax County, New Mexico, are allowed to reach across!"

"I see you've been following the case in the newspapers," said Vail, adding, "The governor and his pals in the incumbent party suspect those half-ass train robberies are the work of some faction out to discredit the machine in charge down yonder. As to which faction, you can take your pick between discontented sheep herding greasers, unreconstructed beef herding rebels, surly coal miners trying to organize a union in defiance of the Colorado Fuel & Iron Company or malcontents laid off recent by the Santa Fe Railroad. Everybody from the governor on down expects the annoying sons of bitches to do it again Friday night–Saturday morn. That gives you four days to crack the case if you get your ass on down to Trinidad on the noon-day Denver & Rio Grande day tripper."

Longarm said, "I can do better than that. There's a freight leaving for El Paso by way of Trinidad earlier if I can be on my damned way, now."

Vail said, "What are you waiting for, a kiss good-bye?"

But old Billy Vail didn't miss much and so as Longarm rose to his full considerable height Vail asked, "What was that about you knotting your tie and getting here early on purpose, old son?"

Longarm grinned down at him through the swirls of tobacco smoke to say, "I was fixing to ask a favor. Seeing

7

as you're sending me out in the field on a fool's errand I don't have to ask it, now."

Vail growled, "The hell you don't. What was it? Spit it out lest you leave me struck with awe and wonder!"

Longarm confessed, "I was fixing to ask you for a few days off, on my own unpaid time, to tend to some personal beeswax."

Vail said, "Mayhaps when you get back. How many days off might we be talking about? I know better than to ask the name of your personal business!"

Longarm shook his head and replied, "Don't need no unpaid time off if you've ordered me out in the field to uphold law and justice. That was about the size of my personal beeswax. I wanted to get out of town 'til that confounded opera about the devil's brother finishes its short but mighty inconvenient run in Denver!"

He moved to the doorway as he added, "We both know the odds on anybody solving shit in four whole days, but tell the governor I tried."

Then he left before Billy Vail could hurl more than a parting curse at him.

In the outer office old Henry, the young cuss who played the typewriter and kept up the files, held out a sheaf of travel orders as Longarm passed his desk. Longarm grabbed them on the fly without asking the obvious but dumb questions as to when old Billy had told the kid to order a senior deputy out in the field. The point was that he was *going* out in the field and all was right with the world again as Longarm moved lightly down the marble stairwell, idly singing . . .

> "On yonder rock, reclining,
> Diavalo waits, a gun in his hand!"

For *Fra Diavalo* wasn't all that bad an opera as long as you didn't have to explain why you were sitting through it with one gal to yet another gal entire. Hence, now, two gals he liked as well, Lord love 'em, were going to enjoy that opera a whole lot better than if he'd been stuck with sitting through it, or trying to, with either of them!

As he headed home to his furnished digs on the less fashionable side of Cherry Creek to change into field duds and gather up his saddle and shit, it had barely entered his mind how neither he nor Billy Vail had even a foggy notion as to what in blue blazes he was supposed to do down Trinidad way, once he got there.

Chapter 2

Longarm had always considered *Black Beauty* a mystery novel. The mystery being how even a gal, growing up in an age of steam and horsepower, ever managed to write such sentimental twaddle about a *horse*.

He'd noticed other hack writers of the she-male persuasion, or possibly men who sat down to pee, went on about the stallion, Traveler, carrying Robert E. Lee through the war, or the more recent Billy the Kid loping all up and down the Pecos aboard that one big gray stud. As a man more inclined to *ride* horses than to keep one as a pet, Longarm knew no serious rider was inclined to get through a working day aboard one particular horse. A horse could carry you thirty or more miles in the course of a whole day if you rode it slow but steady with plenty of trail breaks and all the water it wanted. Once you'd ridden a horse hard for twenty miles or a couple of hours, whichever came first, it was time to swap your saddle to a fresh mount.

So Longarm kept his well broken-in and heavily laden McClellan saddle and bridle in his furnished digs betwixt field jobs and worried about his mount for the moment when the time arose out in the field. Riding out of Denver he usually took what the government wrangler had on hand from their own remuda. Farther off he borrowed government stock off any handy Army post or BIA agency when he could, or hired the most promising stock from local livery stables. There wasn't a town in the world of that sappy *Black Beauty* where they didn't have a livery stable.

Doubting he'd meet up with either President Hayes or his attractive but fussy First Lady, Lemonade Lucy, Longarm shucked the fool tweed suit they expected him to wear on duty but, never knowing what might arise in the field, folded and stored the fussy outfit in one of the saddlebags behind the cantle of his McClellan, under his bedroll with his Winchester '73's boot riding just ahead on the off-side, handy to his free right hand on the trail.

Two empty canteens rode forward, with neither a throw rope nor roping horn between on the fork of a Mc-Clellan, of course.

The saddle, named for a swell garrison soldier who hadn't panned out in combat, had been designed, or copied, by General George McClellan, before the war but after he'd served a hitch as a military attaché in Vienna. If he'd had his way the Union Cav would have ridden into battle mounted on snow white Austrian Lipizzaners, but he'd had to settle for the U.S. War Department accepting his version of an Austro-Hungarian army saddle that had yet to be improved upon for balancing its load comfortably as far as the *horse* was concerned. Being a good rider, Longarm didn't belly-ache as much as some about the discomforts the McClellan offered the rider. A man who wore his pants loose enough to let his nuts get caught in that ventilating slit you were supposed to sit *across*, not *in*, deserved to say ouch until he learned to stand in the damned stirrups at a trot.

Around the Denver District Court or out in the field, Longarm's pan-caked coffee black Stetson and low-heeled army boots went with his badge and guns. But where nobody from Washington was likely to see him he chose to

11

work in the denim work clothes best for a hardscrabble farm back in West-by-God-Virginia or the cattle spreads he'd worked after coming west, before learning they paid even a junior deputy more than a top hand.

Feeling more comfortable already, in clean but faded jeans and a hickory work shirt, Longarm strapped his cross-draw rig back around his horseman's hips and donned the matching blue denim jacket to redistribute the contents of his tweed coat and vest, with some of the shit having to go in shirt pockets, now.

He knew there'd be no call to fill the empty canteens before he got them to Trinidad, and water weighed eight pounds a gallon. For the same reasons he had no call to let a horse go stable-stiff or canteen water to go stagnant in his furnished room betwixt field missions, Longarm was inclined to pick up trail grub where he was headed, rather than carry it before he had to. But he made sure he had a couple of boxes of S&W .44-40 rounds and both his six-gun and saddlegun were chambered before he hefted his combined baggage and set-down to carry on one hip to the railroad yards half a mile away (after locking up and telling his landlady not to mistake any footsteps in his room for mice).

He didn't head for the Union Station at the foot of 17th Street when he'd toted his load across the Larimer Street Bridge. He followed a dirt path along the northwest bank of Cherry Creek to the railroad yards west of the same and headed for the dispatch shed to bum that freight train ride off the D&RGRR.

But the D&RGRR dispatcher, a kindly looking old Dutchman Longarm had never been mad at before, told him "only authorized personnel" were to ride D&RGRR rolling stock until further notice.

When he confided the flap was over those train robberies to the south Longarm tried, "That kid gang has yet to hit *your* line and even if this should be your lucky day,

12

I am the law! Does that sound like unauthorized personnel to you?"

The older man shrugged and said, "I just work here. I don't make the rules. They come down from on high and I'm getting a little old to look for another job."

He looked away with a guilty smile, adding, "I know half the time the big shots giving us orders don't know their asses from their elbows. But ours is not to reason why, like that poem says."

Longarm snorted, "That poem was about six hundred assholes who'd have come out way better if they *had* reasoned why! I need a ride to Trinidad, Dad blast it, and we both know your rolling stock would be safer if I was riding south with it."

The dispatcher said, "You know that and I know that but the board of directors in their infinite wisdom have ordered me not to let anybody on board that ten-forty-five unless employed by the D&RGRR. But, hell, old son, there's that passenger train leaving at noon and so far they ain't said paying passengers can't ride as far as Trinidad."

"That's really funny," Longarm growled, adding, "Just betwixt the two of us, for old times' sake and considering all those holdups took place on a rival rail line's tracks *south* of Trinidad!"

The dispatcher shrugged and said, "That well may be. But don't we meet up with the infernal AT&SFRR at Trinidad and don't our tracks run south in line and within sight of theirs through Raton Pass and as far south as Albuquerque before we wend our separate ways? I'm sorry, Longarm, I feel for you, but I just can't reach you and it ain't as if there wasn't a passenger train leaving at noon!"

Longarm didn't offer the unreasonable old fart a cheroot but managed not to make mention of an older man's mother as he braced the increasingly heavy saddle on his other hip to limp north along the tracks for the back way into the Union Station.

He didn't have to go to the ticket window. He packed a courtesy pass to show any D&RGRR conductor who hadn't heard about him foiling that earlier train robbery south of Trinidad a spell back. Having over an hour to kill and knowing what the candy butchers asked aboard a moving train for stale sandwiches and warm soda pop, Longarm lugged his load out the front and across Wykoop Street to the more reasonable beanery patronized by more seasoned rail travelers.

At an empty corner table, Longarm planted his load out of the way on the floor and sat down to order one of their famous Denver omelets on top of some chili con carne on top of roast beef. He had some long hungry train riding ahead of him that afternoon.

The waitress, who knew him, albeit not in the biblical sense yet, had barely set his order before him when he was joined, uninvited, by a perky spring frock of calico with a mightly shapely form inside it. He didn't mind her sitting down without asking permission. For they sure *did* know one another in the biblical sense and she really liked it dog style as he fondly recalled.

Her name was Freedom Ford. When first they'd met she'd been a part-time newspaper stringer up Leadville way. Now she was a staff reporter for the *Denver Daily Commonwealth*, thanks to the exclusive he'd given her on a domestic tragedy in exchange for her sitting on a federal case for him. Their getting biblical along the way had neither hurt nor helped her career as an up-and-coming western journalist who really knew which end of a cow pony the apples fell from. If only she'd pay attention.

After that, Freedom Ford was one of those demure innocent-looking little things a man had to watch out for once they got him alone. She was shaped like a well-built teenager and wore her coffee-with-cream hair up under a Paris hat she'd have never been able to manage when first they'd met up Leadville way. He didn't ask her if she knew she had a dead bluebird on her head. She had

14

to know, once she'd paid that much for any hat.

She announced in that lofty tone women used when greeting old lovers they hadn't been screwing lately, "It's so good to see you again, Custis. Is it safe to assume I might have another exclusive, if you are on your way to where I assume you must be on your way?"

Longarm signaled the waitress as he soberly replied, "I got a bone to pick with you about that last exclusive I gave you, Miss Freedom."

She flittered her lashes to purr, "I love it when you get a boner for me, Custis!"

He laughed depite himself and said, "So do it. But you had no call to make that modest shoot-out in the Carbonate Spa Wine Theater read like Pickett's charge up Missionary Ridge, for Pete's sake. I only shot that one sneak as he was fixing to back-shoot me on those stairs. His round meant for me nailed the two-faced woman I'd been following up the stairs like a moon calf. Your story made it seem I'd shot it out with the James-Younger gang at Northfield and got 'em all!"

She shrugged her trim shoulders and made mention of poetic license.

As the waitress joined them Longarm asked the newspaper gal what she'd have. Freedom allowed she'd just have one donut with her coffee because she had to watch her weight. The waitress, who outweighed her by thirty pounds, shot her a murderous look but said she'd fetch her order.

As she flounced off Freedom asked, "So what's the story on those train robberies down in Raton Pass, where both the Santa Fe and the Denver and Rio Grande pass through those Sangre de Cristo Mountains, dear?"

Wanting to know what else she'd heard wrong, Longarm gently but firmly explained, "Raton Pass don't cut through the Sangre de Cristos. It ain't that dramatic by half. The D&RGRR naturally runs south along the front ranges. The AT&SFRR naturally turns south, the same as

15

the old Santa Fe Trail it follows west, when it gets sort of bumpy at Trinidad. The trail and both newer railroads run south down the east flanks of the Sangre de Cristos to get *around* that swamping fault block a hundred and twenty miles south of the New Mexico line. That's what you call a fifty or sixty mile-across strip of extinct sea bottom shoved way in the middle of the air. A fault block. Them mountains run north and south, west of Trinidad and Raton Pass. Raton Pass runs over the rocky-enough but way *lower* divide between the Purgatoire and Canadian rivers, see?"

She nodded knowingly and decided, "Purgatoire is the way Mexicans say Purgatory and Trinidad means Trinity, right?"

The waitress served Freedom her coffee, another dirty look, and a donut glazed with chocolate and grated peanuts, since the little snip had only ordered *one* and it just wasn't *fair*!

Longarm said, "Trinidad got its start as a failed Spanish mission to the Comanche, Kiowa, and such to wind up the last stop on the Santa Fe Trail before Raton Pass. Mex sheepmen from Santa Fe and later cattle men coming up the Goodnight Trail from Texas both herded their stock over Raton Pass to graze the fertile foothills Trinidad nestles in."

Freedom left her decadent donut where the waitress had put it as she sipped her coffee thoughtfully and said, "I read something about Anglo cattlemen and Mex sheep herders having a real bella roar down that way in, when, '69?"

He said, "Close. But no cigar. The Animas County War betwixt factions led by Cattle Baron Frank Bloom and Sheep Baron Felipe Baca came to a hot head in '67, *before* the wedding of the rails. Like that more recent Lincoln County War, the Animas County War scared the big shots who started it back to their senses as it commenced to get out of hand. Nobody has ever come up with certain

16

casualty figures for the day-long Battle of Trinidad but as the smoke cleared, unlike the Murphy-Dolan-Ryan or the Chisum-Tunstall-McSween factions down Lincoln County way, the Anglo and Mex survivors around Trinidad declared an armistice as the gunsmoke was still clearing."

He washed down some of his more substantial order and went on to say, "The stockmen down yonder had an incentive for a lasting peace the ones further south still lack. First, prospectors searching for the gold those early Spaniards had never found struck *coal*, a *heap* of coal just to the northwest of Trinidad in '73. Both the D&RGRR and AT&SFRR arrived forthwith to carry the tonnage away. Such tonnage being dug out from under the foothills by neither Anglo nor Mex riders, but by imported *furriners* who soon outnumbered hell out of the original settlers and, as we speak, a whole *Nuevo Trinidad* is growing like a weed, or a cancer, northwest of what the old-timers now call *Corazon de Trinidad.*"

She brightened and said, "That means the *heart* of Trinidad, right? Who do you think is going to win the election down there this fall, dear, the Republican machine that's been running things or those Irish and Dago Democrats not even the mine owners seem to have any control over?"

To which Longarm could only confess he had no idea. When she asked if he thought those otherwise pointless milk train robberies could be the work of political radicals he said they were sending him down that way to ask. She demurely asked if he had time to "See her home" before his train left and it sure beat all how tempting a sure thing could be after you'd had time to recover from the last time it had commenced to feel a tad like a chore to get it up again.

He suspected she was feeling the same stirrings in her loins and, what the hell he could always catch a later train.

But the difference bewixt a man on duty and a kid with

a hard-on was the man knowing he could always get laid again, sooner or later, after he had carried out his damned duty. So they parted friendly, with a French kiss on the platform as a matter of fact. But he perforce had to ask Freedom if he could look her up and tell her more once he got back from Trinidad and she showed she was a grown-up by smiling gamely and vowing she meant to question him thoroughly.

Longarm was already regretting his devotion to duty by the time he was on board with his McClellan. For he faced one hell of a tedious afternoon ride with a raging erection that wasn't going to feel any better as he thought back to that last night in Leadville with Freedom, whether or not he wanted to.

Then he asked the gal seated under an empty stretch of baggage rack whether she'd mind his load up yonder. When she replied in a friendly way that she wouldn't mind at all, he took a second look at her and decided he might as well sit down beside her if she didn't mind. And when she said she wouldn't mind at all he forgot all about the one he'd just let get away, for *this* one was just plain bodacious!

Chapter 3

The Junoesque blue-eyed brunette looked to be either side
of thirty and in a remarkable state of good health. Being
a woman of some quality she was naturally wearing a tan
travel duster over her well-filled-out bodice of pleated
lavender silk. You could still tell because she hadn't but-
toned up the top of her duster whilst the train was standing
in the station. It got hot along the floodplain of the South
Platte at noon by late May.

For the same reasons you could see her shiny black
hair and flawless ivory features because she had yet to
lower the travel veil of her broad brimmed summer straw.
From the way she smiled when Longarm introduced himself she seemed to like what she saw as well. So instead
of facing a five or six hour forever on a passenger local
he found himself hoping five or six hours was going to
be long enough. Or whether she'd be getting off at Trinidad or riding on out of his life to Lord only knew where.

But before their adventure even started they'd established her name was Alda Grey and there'd been all that
room on the baggage rack above them because she had
her own bags and a whole slew of insurance papers up in
the baggage car ahead. Better yet, she'd be getting off at
Trinidad with them and might need some help with them,

seeing as she'd never been there before and hadn't the least notion how the town was laid out.

She said she was a bookkeeper for a Denver insurance firm that had been taking a beating over those mysterious milk train robberies he was on his way to look into, speaking of small worlds.

When he asked how come, with a puzzled smile, Alda explained how, even though nothing of value had been taken from one train, milk had to show up at the dairy contracting for it by the time agreed to if the agreed on price was to be paid in full.

Longarm frowned thoughtfully and asked, "Hold on, Miss Alda, are you saying the dairy in town turned all that milk down flat, or did they take delivery at a *lower price*?"

She said, "The latter, and there's no argument the cheap rascals were taking advantage of the few hours' delay. Dairy farmers all along the milk train's morning route were offered half price for their fresh milk, take it, or offer rapidly *spoiling* milk somewhere *else*. Before you ask me, no, they did not pass the savings on to their customers. Milk unloaded a little late in the wee small hours went out across town with their milkmen at the usual time, or at any rate not late enough for the housewives of Trinidad to notice."

The train jerked into motion under them, throwing her shoulder against his denim-clad arm. He didn't mind. He said, "That seems pretty raw. And it's the first motive for slowing down milk deliveries I've heard, so far. Your insurance company is involved . . . in what way, ma'am? All them homesteaders along the route took out policies with you against train robbers?"

She lowered the travel veil as she sighed, "Of course not. The *railroad* is insured with us and since all those outraged farmers are suing the same line to recover their losses, with the railroad settling out of court and passing their losses on to us . . ."

"I follow your drift," Longarm cut in. He knew better than to ask how much money they were talking about. He didn't want her clamming up on him, as witnesses tended to when you asked about their sex lives or finances. Further along, like the old church song suggested, would be plenty of time for exact figures if exact figures mattered.

The notion that a sinister band of Trinidad milk men were stopping the milk trains *once a week* to get a bargain on their daily deliveries got sort of far-fetched as one studied on it.

So they settled back to tell one another the stories of their lives and sip the warm soda pop he ordered anyway, as experienced fellow travelers aboard a pokey local passenger train puffing ever southward along the aprons of the front ranges, with the scenery to their east less interesting rolling prairie, albeit greened up and bespangled with wild flowers that early in the year after a fairly wet spring. After noon, the mountains off to their west kept getting more purple as the day wore on. You had to get up early to see the Blood of Christ along the far-off ridges as you got well south of Denver. North of, say, Colorado Springs, or well into the afternoon, the red sandstone they'd named the Sangre de Cristos for had yet to aspire that high up the eastern flanks of what they called the Rampart Range. When they seemed to run out of mountain to the west entirely near Pueblo, Alda naturally asked what had happened.

Like others, she'd been told to watch for the Blood of Christ high in the sky down this way.

Longarm explained, "We're crossing the east-west floodplains of the Arkansas River, Miss Alda. It busts out of its Royal Gorge out of sight to the west to lay everything lower in these parts. We'll be picking up the lower Wet Mountains a ways south and they'll turn into hogbacks of the Sangre de Cristos as they swing over the horizon from the west into view. Ought to be able to make 'em out just south of the jerkwater stop at Walsenberg.

The very crest of the Sangre de Cristos rises fifty miles or more west of Trinidad and so only the higher peaks show above the way closer mesas and hogbacks. There's some argument as to whether Spanish Peak, closer to town, is a peak of the Sangre de Cristos or a last gasp of the Wet Mountains."

She said the geology of the Rocky Mountains sounded more complicated than it looked on a picture postcard.

He nodded soberly and said, "We keep trying to tell the big shots in Washington that when they ask how come whole tribes of Indians, let alone train robbers, manage to hide out from us in a mountain maze that's over four hundred miles across in places. Something awful happened long ago to create an awful lot of bumps before the rains of a few million years carved it up so curious they ain't done mapping all of it yet."

"Is that why the Animas County posses haven't been able to catch those milk train robbers?" she demanded.

It was a dumb question. But she was pretty. So Longarm patiently explained, "We're talking a good lead under cover of darkness before any posse could start after anybody. Everybody seems to suspect the outlaws went to ground somewhere west of the tracks on higher ground. I scouted Mister Lo, the poor Indian, for the army across open plains a spell back. So I'm keeping my options open. I know everybody says they lost track of those four mystery riders on higher range. I once topped a prairie rise to spy a whole Cheyenne village hidden in a draw along with a gallery forest of cottonwood that wasn't on any map. Trinidad nestles betwixt carved up mesas north and south with that mighty rolling Raton Divide just to the south of the stretch they've chosen to stage those dramatic but pointless holdups. I mean to be on board, with that saddle and Winchester above us on my own mount, come next Friday, unless I get lucky, earlier."

She asked, "Oh, dear, do you think they mean to strike again?"

He said, "If I don't catch 'em sooner. They've hit the same milk train three weekends running. They must have some reason and we got us one more Friday night–Saturday morn at the end of this month."

They got to kill almost forty-five minutes gnawing that bone. But after they'd agreed there was just no sensible answer and she declined his offer of another warm soda pop they lapsed into silence for a spell.

It didn't hurt. Alda Grey was good company whether she was going on about outlaws and insurance or not. He was pleased to see she wasn't one of those gals who couldn't stand silent intervals and had to fill them in with gossip about Queen Victoria and her Scotch butler or whether old Professor Darwin was on to something or just *loco en la cabeza*.

After a while, since he asked, she explained she'd been told to check in to the new Columbian Hotel near Commercial and Main Streets, wherever that might be, and await further instructions. She said she was supposed to deliver all those papers to a claims adjuster headed west aboard the AT&SFRR from their Chicago affiliates.

Longarm had planned on checking into the older and less expensive Trinidad House just down the way. But what the hell, it wasn't all that much less expensive. So he said he'd be switched if he wasn't headed for the Columbian Hotel his ownself and asked her how heavy a load she had to move there from the depot, adding, "Our hotel's about eight hundred yards south of the depot on the north bank of the river in Nuevo Trinidad. We got to get you and your baggage to the center of things in Corazon de Trinidad, which is still the civilized third of town. Everything thrown up by the mining interests north of the river is a glorified shanty town. Main Street in the older parts resulted from paving a section of the old Santa Fe Trail with gravel. Commercial Street resulted from the Goodnight Cattle Trail coming up from the south to meet the same. They asked both railroads to sort of swing around the business district. So they both do, sharing the same depot, with the AT&SFRR following the north bank of the river to swing south across the same, west of town."

She allowed it sounded confusing and said she had forty or more pounds of papers along with her own over-night bags. He said in that case they'd hire a hack for the short but overloaded drive to the Columbian. She said she was certainly glad she'd met up with someone who knew his way around Trinidad. It would have sounded dumb to say *he* was just as glad she was. So he never said it.

It sounded more mature to ask her if there might be any other insurance claims resulting from those otherwise pointless early morning holdups. She said she hadn't heard tell of any, since no rolling stock nor train crewmen had been damaged. The railroad was self-insured as far as that fire on their tracks went. No private underwriters, including Lloyds of London, could have insured thousands of miles of unguarded tracks or cross ties for any premiums any railroad stockholders were about to pay.

Longarm asked other questions as dumb, lest she steer the conversation back to biography. He'd told her all she needed to know about himself. A gal had the right to know whether a fellow traveler was married up or wanted by the law. They'd already established she was a grass widow who'd gone back to work after divorcing a hand-some compulsive gambler who just couldn't win and wouldn't quit. He didn't *want* to know about other men who might have used and abused her until she needed assurances he wasn't another no-good love-'em-and-leave-'em brute. That was where gals seemed to be headed with such sob stories, unless they were just brag-ging. The idea was to shut the tap off before they told you too much. Some women seemed to feel a man owed them vows of eternal respect after they told him how they'd been pistol whupped and corn-holed by a rascal they'd been dumb enough to trust. Even assuring a gal you had no intention of pistol whupping or corn-holing her could get them started on dreams of ivy covered cottages once they talked you into getting a better job.

But old Alda, wonder of wonders, seemed content to talk about milk train robberies or comment on the passing scenery as they rode on long enough to feel like pals. She seemed to really give a shit when Longarm pointed at smoke rising above a mesa to their west and told her, "That chimney haze, yonder, would be Ludlow. Company town built by the Colorado Fuel and Iron Company above a soft coal seam. So we're only about a dozen miles from Trinidad, now."

She asked how many coal miners might be living closer to Trinidad, adding, "I understand there was small need for morning milk there until all those immigrants and their families moved in."

He said, "Most cattle and sheep outfits keep a few milch cows handy for the cream in their coffee. The coal companies are still bringing them in off the docks back east. Italian, Irish, and Greek, in that order, down this way. They say Welshmen know more about mining coal. But Welshmen have been mining coal long enough to talk back when the boss puts production ahead of safety."

She asked if they'd had any labor troubles in the Colorado coal fields, repressing a shudder as she harked back to the Molly Maguire terrorists in the eastern collieries.

He said, "Not around Trinidad, so far. Few Colorado coal mines have been operating long enough to attract organized labor. I was on a job that we *thought* was a western version of the Molly Maguires a spell back, but it was trouble stirred up by crooks out to rob a bank in the end and not all that close to Trinidad in any case. I figure it ought to take the miners down this way another generation to notice they're *American* working stiffs who owe their souls to the company store. The first generation is usually too pleased to be working out this way instead of where they came from. The boss is always going to take advantage of you. Some American bosses can be real . . . bossy. But from what I've heard tell, the worse we have can't hold a candle to the bosses those green immigrants got *away* from."

She started to ask, then decided on her own it made no sense for labor agitators to mess with the morning milk deliveries. She'd heard, however, of the newer machine in Trinidad putting up an Italian-Irish-Greek slate against the county incumbents, come November.

Longarm allowed he'd heard the same and added it was too soon to tell if that meant anything as far as the case they were both concerned about mattered. They fell pleasantly silent and then their train pulled into the Trinidad depot and they were too busy to bullshit until after they had her heavier load and his saddle checked into adjoining rooms at the high-toned Columbian Hotel at Main and Commercial.

By the time they had, and she was out of that travel duster to turn out more shapely than he'd imagined, Longarm told her he had to get on up to Firehouse One to pay his expected courtesy call on the the local law.

She smiled uncertainly and asked, "Firehouse One, Custis?"

He explained, "Efficiency. They explained it to me the last time I passed through. Once they'd built their swell two-story brick firehouse up closer to the depot they noticed how much grander it was than any of their other municipal offices. So they moved the town marshal in on the floor above the fire department and put jail cells in the basement under the same. If you commit arson in Trinidad you wind up under the engine they use to put your fire out. I got time to let the town law know I'm in town and I still might make it over to the county seat to log in with the sheriff's department. Once I have, seeing it'll be too late in the day for much else, I'll be proud to take you to supper as soon as I get back."

She suggested they order room service and asked him

if he thought she had time to take a bath before she changed into evening wear.

He said he'd likely be an hour or more and they'd already noticed the new hotel had indoor plumbing with adjoining baths. So she told him not to hurry and he said he liked to dine after sundown, too.

This was not, in fact, his usual habit unless supping with Hispanic ladies, inclined to eat as late as eight or nine. But if he was following her drift she meant to serve him some clean-indeed dessert and it didn't seem decent to shove a room service supper out of the way and head for the nearby bed before the cool shades of evening made this seem more romantic.

Chapter 4

Firehouse Number One was at 314 North Commercial, above Main and hence handier to trouble in what was now going on in half of Trinidad, north of the river and Santa Fe tracks. It was well after five and the chief had left for the day. But it was the thought that counted and so Longarm introduced himself to the desk sergeant on the second floor and signed their blotter or daily log. He still had a sheriff to call on but it wouldn't have been polite to sign and run. So he accepted the usual snort from the filing cabinet and set a spell to jaw about the mysterious milk train robberies.

A couple of Trinidad detectives joined in. One of the first things Longarm learned was that *they'd* been kicking around the notion about a plot to make a dishonest profit on the morning milk deliveries.

When Longarm pointed out they were only talking about one morning a week, so far, a know-it-all who could have lost a good forty pounds with no injury to his health opined, "We figure it tallies to better than a thousand a week. Can't get the dairy crew to furnish precise figures but beat all them farmers down on a couple of thousand dollars worth of fresh milk and we ain't just whistling Dixie!"

Longarm said, "I was just talking to someone as works for an insurance company about that and you're right, up to a point."

He let that sink in before he added, "Let's say the mastermind is in the milk delivery business and his master plan is to skim the cream off the Saturday morn delivery . . ."

The desk sergeant chimed in, "You mean Saturday, Sunday, Monday. They don't deliver every morning to the same address. They cover alternated routes, dropping off a quart or more every other day. That was the excuse the dairy used when it refused to pay full price for late farm produce."

The fat detective explained, "They allowed they could only deliver half before it was time to make cottage cheese out of the rest. So the Friday deliveries went as usual. Nobody got nothing on Saturday and of course there's no deliveries anywhere on the Sabbath. So . . ."

"So you just shot that notion off the fence," Longarm cut in with a weary smile, adding, "The dairy here in town *did* have an excuse to cut prices without passing them on. Like the outraged farmers along that milk train's route, they lost money on the deal themselves and, after that, consider how much a devious dairy would have to pay four masked riders to do the dirty deed. We're talking hard time in Canyon City no matter what they think they're doing."

The fat detective asked, "All right, Uncle Sam, what do *you* think them four are doing?"

To which Longarm could only reply, "I don't have the least notion. I came down here to see if I could find out. I mean to poke around Trinidad asking questions for the next few days, with your approval, and unless I get somewhere on foot I mean to be aboard that milk train come Friday night with my Winchester and a sudden horse."

They told him they'd heard the same plan from the county law and said they meant to have some of their own riders patrolling the tracks at least an hour's ride south of town.

Longarm said in that case he'd best have a word with their sheriff and nobody tried to stop him from leaving.

The county courthouse was closer to Maple and Main, just a spit and a whistle from the old Spanish Santa Trinidad or Holy Trinity Church the town had grown up around. Being Anglo, the courthouse was balloon frame. They kept talking about erecting something more imposing built of brick or even sandstone, but so far they'd kept things pragmatic.

Longarm found the sheriff long gone and the deputy holding the fort overnight less interesting to talk to. So once he'd signed in and told them where he could be found if they needed him before morning he was free to head on back to the Columbian and order supper from room service.

When he got there and knocked on Alda Grey's door next to his own, he found she'd already had them bring the rolling table up with a brace of menus and a carafe of white Bordeaux, which she declared her favorite in a mighty casual tone, considering.

For the first thing he'd noticed when she opened her door to him was her notion of evening wear. She seemed to feel a casually worn kimono of hemp-colored shantung was formal enough for a room service supper in a hotel room as the sun was commencing to set outside.

She hadn't lit the oil lamps but the candles on the table were aglow. So he could see she wore silk slippers on her feet but nothing else at all under that floor length kimono. You could tell when a gal was bare-ass under thin shantung, even when it didn't tend to gap some above and below the obi sash.

The table was set up near the open window, facing the sunset. Longarm hung up his jacket, hat and gunbelt as Alda showed him how up-to-date the Columbian was by pulling a cord on the wall of the niche her made-up bed reposed in. She said their waiter would be coming up to take their orders and that she'd already figured out what *she* was having for supper.

So Longarm sat down to read the menu, noting the light from the nearby window was still bright, even as it made the cream paper look like orange peel.

Being the fancy new hotel didn't want its guest to consider it slow, the menu was loaded with fancy French terms for grub. But Longarm had ate refined before and knew *pommes frites* were French fries and the last time he'd ordered *bifteck* it had turned out to be steak. He didn't want any rabbit food and they didn't seem to have any . . . Oh, sure, *chili avec viande* was likely how a Frog said chili con carne. He told Alda he'd go along with her on dessert. He could only hope she knew what she was doing when she allowed in that case he'd be having some *blanc-mange* with her.

They'd just worked that out when the snooty waiter showed up, pretending not to notice Longarm was in hickory and denim whilst Alda was closer to naked. He just took their orders and, seeing he really spoke English, was a sport about Longarm ordering black coffee with his meal in the same, and turned to fetch their grub. Before he could get out the door Alda said they could use more wine. So the poker-faced son of a bitch allowed he understood and left 'em alone some more as, outside, the other buildings all around turned purple and gold under the dying embers of the sunset's sky.

Alda sipped more wine and asked if he didn't find their room service supper more "atmospheric" than going out to a restaurant might have turned out. He could see by the contents of the clear glass bottle she hadn't had enough wine, waiting for him, to sound that atmospheric. He was just as glad. A gal who'd convinced herself she was a tad uninhibited was one thing. It was a pain in the ass when they passed out on you.

Sipping some white Bordeaux, himself, lest she take

him for a sissy, he told her about his conversations with other lawmen and asked if she could offer an educated guess as to just how much those three holdups in a row might cost her insurance underwriters.

She shook her head, inspiring another lock of loosely bound brown hair to spill down the front of her as she said, "I'd have to go over all the premiums. But it won't be too much to bear, thanks to the way we've spread the risk. That affiliate claims adjuster I told you about works for yet another firm we share the spread with. I know it sounds complicated when you don't know the insurance game, but . . ."

"I know a little," he cut in, adding, "This English gal investigating claims for Lloyds of London explained how Lloyds of London ain't the big insurance company it looks like. It started in a London coffeehouse when a whole posse of independent insurance underwriters got together to pool their risks. Anyone can see how one insurance outfit could be wiped out by some natural disaster sinking a whole fleet of insured ships or killing off a whole bunch of life insurance policy holders. So when anybody insures anything with Lloyds of London he really chooses one of dozens of firms operating under the Lloyds umbrella. He knows they'll always be able to pay off because each underwriter chips in to a general slush fund insuring *them* in turn from having to pay out more than they have in their own till."

Alda nodded owlishly and said, "That's about the size of it, albeit we only spread our American risks among a more modest syndicate of what the general public views as friendly rivals. Was she . . . nice to talk to in bed, Custis?"

Longarm quietly replied, "I don't recall saying anything about that insurance lady and me in bed, Miss Alda."

She dimpled in the dim light to reply, "Didn't you? Funny, it sounded as if you were repeating pillow talk.

32

Were you questioning her in a back room with a bar of soap in a sock?"

Longarm had to laugh at the picture. That pretty little English gal had actually been on top whilst explaining how Lloyds of London insured ships and such. But since it was against his code to kiss and tell, he told the curious American gal, "As a matter of fact the conversation got started aboard another train." And this was the simple truth up to them getting off together in Salt Lake City to continue their conversation.

It didn't work. Alda nodded knowingly and murmured, "Reminds me of people we know. But let's not worry about ladies whose secrets seem to be so safe with you. I wonder where that damned waiter is right now. I hate it when the help walks in on you just as . . . never mind."

He softly suggested, "You'd best go easy on that wine until you get something for it to land on, inside."

She said, "I am not!" and he knew she was funning when she went on to lisp, "Some thinkle peep I'm under the alcaflunce of inkahol. But I won't dare what theeple pink."

Then their waiter knocked once and came in with their grub on a rolling dolly without waiting to be told they weren't at it yet.

Alda pulled herself together as he served and calmly told him they'd have no further use for room service for now. When he asked about the dessert they'd ordered she told him they'd decided to pass on the *blanc-mange*. The waiter said he didn't blame them, added the meal would be added to their bill and silently thanked Longarm for the silver dollar on the tablecloth with a nod as he made it vanish.

When he left, Alda said Longarm had overtipped him. Longarm shrugged and said, "When in Rome. I understand the governor and his lady stay here when they're down this way and the help don't gossip as much about those who take care of them. A good sport is a trade secret to be treasured."

She smiled knowingly and said, "I could see right off you were a well-traveled man of the world. Do we really have to go through the charade of downing all this food when that's not what we're really hungry for? I don't want this excuse for French *cuisine* inside me, Custis. You *know* what I want inside me, and I'm not talking about anybody putting anything in my *stomach*!"

So Longarm rose and as she came up to meet him in the gathering dusk it seemed only natural to serve her some French kissing before he swept her up and carried her on over to that inviting bed niche.

She had a head start on him, since she only had to shuck her kimono, so they came the first time with his jeans around the ankles of his army boots and his hickory shirt open down the front but thankfully protecting his back, some, from her nails as she sobbed between wet kisses about how long it had been since the last time she'd had that much manhood in her. He figured she was likely bending the long bow to make him feel good, but that was fair. He was lying through his teeth when he assured her she was the best thing that had ever happened to him. It was a *white* lie and as a matter of fact old Alda was tight, or knew how to make it tight for a gal as curvaceous and obviously experienced as all that.

Once they'd calmed down to where he could get all the way undressed he wanted more of the same, with his bare feet against the footboard so as to offer more serious and faster thrusts as he warned her to retract those tigress claws for Pete's sake.

He doubted he'd be out in the field long enough for serious claw marks to heal and some of his Denver pals liked it in front of a mirror by lamp light, bless their dirty little minds.

By the time he'd inspired Alda to come three times it was just about totally dark in her bed niche, with only a

34

square of street glow from outside on the pressed tin ceiling. So she asked if they could have more light on the subject when he wheeled that rolling room service table over by the bed.

He groped in the dark for his duds and found a waterproof Mex match to relight the candles the window draft had blown out earlier. Over by the bed niche they both burned steadier and brighter. Alda said they made her feel romantic. They were both feeling hungry enough after all that passion to enjoy cooled off but not-bad grub. They sat side by side with their bare feet on the floor and bare hips touching as they wined and dined some, but wound up leaving half the grub on their plates as they somehow wound up with him still seated at the table with her on her knees under it, serving him French delicacies indeed as he finished his black coffee. A man drank such black coffee as he could manage when he knew it was fixing to be a long night.

Before midnight he suspected old Alda was just showing off. He knew *he* was as they went at it dog style for the second time. Having learned the hard way not to reach for the impossible, Longarm just kept humping away without trying to come, figuring sooner or later she would, or she'd say she had, and what the hell, you could keep it halfway hard if you were in good shape and just kept moving it, idly wondering why.

Longarm was a considerate lover who liked women, as fellow sufferers of an unjust fate. He knew men and women both deserved something better than one another and he'd learned to make the best of a bad situation by understanding and adjusting to the physical limitations of fornication.

Unlike all too many natural men who naturally felt like turning over to go to sleep once they'd had enough, Longarm gamely accepted the facts of life as they'd been dealt out by Dame Nature, or what Professor Darwin called his evolution. She-male critters in heat had evolved to fuck

35

all the he-males in the pack and it was nobody's fault but Queen Victoria and fussy church elders that folk were supposed to pair off one on one, more romantic. So a man had to do what a man had to do, even if those same laws of evolution made a man who'd been a raging bull a tad earlier in the evening wonder what all the fuss was about as he stared down at his fool organ grinder sliding in and out with as much passion as he'd have felt watching a steam piston until she gasped, "I'm sorry! I just can't take any more, dear! You have me too sensitized to bear!"

So he took mercy on her and they shared a smoke, propped up on the pillows, talking about milk trains and such until they'd finished two cheroots and *damn* her tits looked lovely by candlelight and why had he ever taken it out, that last time, without coming in such a tight little ring-dang-doo?

"What are you laughing about, dear?" Alda asked as she snuggled closer.

He said, "Dame Nature. Ain't she a bitch when you study on it?"

Chapter 5

Ben Franklin had been right about getting to bed early making for early rising. So next morning just at sunrise Longarm slipped into his own room next door to fuss up the bedding and use the soap and towels in the adjoining bath, letting some slopped shaving lather lay where it had landed on the tile floor as Alda still lay slugabed, as if she'd been the one doing all the work.

The Corazon de Trinidad was a compact grid of around ten by twelve city blocks, but farther out it commenced to sprawl and there were limits to how much ground a man could cover afoot. So Longarm packed his saddle and bridle to a nearby livery on Convent Street and killed two birds with one stone whilst he jawed about horseflesh and politics with the old Mexican running the operation.

Once he'd explained he needed a steady plodder who could get him around town and stand tethered from time to time without creating a fuss, the older man selected a no-longer-young cordovan barb mare with nice lines, allowing she was still a high-stepper no *caballero* should feel ashamed to be seen on, whilst still calmed down enough for tedious errands.

As they saddled and bridled her together Longarm explained who he was, what he was there for, and casually asked who the local Mexicans favored in the coming elections.

The older man shrugged and replied, *"Son nada más segunderas.* They are all no more than shits to us! The usual Anglo shits, other shits from yet other places we have never heard of. Why should we wish for to vote for any of them, eh?"

Longarm asked if they'd ever considered running one of their own for public office.

The Mexican sighed and said, "Back as late as 1867 there was talk of *la raza* taking charge of a *barrio* we *Hombres de la Santa Fe* first settled in the teeth of *Los Comanches.* But the cost in blood was too high when we counted our dead while the gunsmoke cleared. I mean no disrespect. I know who you are and they say you are a man of sympathy, *El Brazo Largo*, but your people do not make war in a logical manner. Did you know *all* the land this far west used to belong to Mexico?"

Longarm allowed he'd heard as much.

The older man said, "Is true. At El Alamo our great general, Santa Ana, won the battle and killed every Gringo, save for an Anglo woman, her child and a servant he spared so that she could carry news of his victory and a warning not to trifle with him to the rest of you."

Gently but firmly forcing the mare to accept the curb bit and buckling the cheekpiece to fit, the older man sighed and said, "Your people never listen. Was like trying for to step on ants and the next thing we knew we were all in *Los Estados Unidos* all the way out to California. So we how-you-say try to get along and we have found is more better not to attract Anglo attention to our ways by making speeches. Our ways are not your ways, especially here along the Sangre de Cristos and perhaps I have said enough."

Longarm didn't argue the point. He knew how peculiar some Mexicans found certain customs along the Sangre de Cristos, where the old time mixture of Roman Catholic and Pagan Indian notions had blended into a sort of rival of the Afro-Roman voodoo notions over on the Gulf. As far as Colorado or New Mexican statute law went, the outlandish cult known as *Los Penitentes* wasn't supposed to happen. No Pope in Rome had ever approved the notion of nailing men and boys to crosses to prove they were just as Christian as the original Christ.

Most members of the cult itself, in point of fact, lacked the balls to try for that much personal holiness. So they had awestruck respect for those now-holy illiterate breeds who'd volunteered to be crucified.

Volunteer was the operative words as far as Longarm was concerned. He had brushed with Los Penitentes in the past and discovered that as in the case of all seriously religious folk, you got a mixture of frothing at the mouth fanatics and those who meant well. For all their odd notions about salvation, Los Penitentes seemed to mostly mean well and, when they weren't nailing one another to crosses, they were famed for being nice to less fortunate Mexicans and even others down on their luck. During the great depression of the early seventies food baskets and other hand-outs from the sort of spooky cult had meant the difference for many a hungry family along both slopes of the Sangre de Cristos. The cultists, themselves, seemed to be headquartered somewhere up amid the blood-red crags. Nobody knew for certain. When you asked two Mexicans about Los Penitentes you got three answers.

Longarm had a time picturing those mystery riders nailing one another to crosses when they weren't stopping milk trains. So he mounted up. Her name seemed to be Caramelo so he decided to call her Candy, and rode out to the west to get his bearings on the local railroading.

He hadn't ridden a mile before he saw that as he recalled from less tighter inspection, just passing through, most every route through town from the north or east tended to bottleneck southwest of Corozon de Trinidad.

The Purgatoire wound up from the southwest. Main

Street followed the older course of the Santa Fe Trail to swing southeast as well where it met the river a few vacant lots west of High Street. Longarm knew, without riding that far south, how the old Goodnight Trail swung off to the east from the rambles of the Santa Fe to enter Corazon de Trinidad as Commercial Street. He and Candy splashed across the stirrup-deep Purgatoire to the railroad tracks beyond.

Reining in to stare southwest through the morning haze, Longarm saw how the rival AT&SFRR and D&RGRR lines followed the flood terrace of the river out of sight that way. He swung Candy's head northeast to follow the tracks into the can of worms behind the depot used by both railroads.

As in the case of insurance companies and rival nations, railroads were inclined to make war or cut deals as the situations seemed to call for. The legendary shooting war betwixt the rail crews of the Santa Fe and the Denver & Rio Grande in the Royal Gorge to the north was a gory chapter in recent Colorado history, with the pistoleers of the Denver & Rio Grande winning their route up the Royal Gorge at gunpoint and still inclined to crow about it.

Down this way, forced by the lay of the land to get along better, they got along better, sharing a consolidated switch yard as well as the only depot in town. Longarm knew how, farther south where Raton Pass was too wide for one side or the other to hold against all comers, the way the D&RGRR had forted up in the Royal Gorge, the tracks ran side by side, each a single line, but resembling a two-track line to the casual eye. Western Union had strung its lines between and then, of course, each rail line had its own telegraph line, making things look more settled than they really were along the eastern flanks of the Sangre de Cristos until they parted company down Albuquerque way to the *west* of the same.

Squiring Alda and her baggage from the depot the day

before Longarm had noticed the new Harvey House alongside the tracks. The Santa Fe trains didn't have Pullman diners like some of the bigger lines. But old Fred Harvey, an Englishman with an imagination, had talked them into letting him set up trackside beaneries where the service was usually fast and the coffee was always good, considing old Fred was a limey.

Longarm had missed breakfast in order to get started. He rode on just the same, reining in by a dispatch shed to get down and share some smoke and bullshit with a cuss who said he worked for the AT&SFRR.

The dispatcher was an Irishman of about forty, missing a right hand. You found out right away he'd lost his hand at Cold Harbor, not no fucking railroad accident, because he told you this before you could light his cheroot for him.

After that he didn't know much about those milk trains they'd been holding up to the southwest. His beeswax, he said his name was Corrigan, was seeing the considerable freight of Trinidad off to the northeast. He confirmed, as Longarm had already surmised, the community of less than ten thousand was shipping bodacious tonnage. Mostly soft coal, these days, with enough beef and mutton on the hoof or wool, hides and tallow, in that order of value, in quantities to matter.

Longarm speculated and the railroad man agreed the local stockmen had come out ahead once the iron horse had reached them and of course homesteaders producing raw milk, fresh eggs, pigs, chickens and truck for the ever expanding population had no reason to hate the folk who ran their early morning milk trains.

Corrigan opined, "All that guff about the James boyos fighting the railroad to be after helping the poor is a bucket of blather and, sure, I've heard that on the Missouri Pacific they keep robbing runs nowhere near that old homestead they weep so much about and all."

Longarm nodded soberly and said, "The Glendale train

they robbed more recently runs through the far parts of the Missouri they claim they aim to protect from the greedy rail barons. But some old boys like to have some excuse when they pull a holdup. Takes a man who ain't afraid to look at his fool self in the mirror to just decide it seems a swell day to stick a gun in somebody's face because he'd rather rob folk than get a job. As a lawman I have more respect for a crook who faces up to what he really is."

He took a thoughtful drag on his own cheroot before he recalled, "I was transporting convicts one time when the subject came up. This horse thief who was still shaving every other day smirked about us convicting him for for *borrowing* a horse from the Army Remount Service. This older con we had in the same wagon cussed him out as a disgrace to an old if dishonorable profession. He told the punk a horse thief that wasn't man enough to describe himself as a *thief* was still a smirksome moon calf no sincere outlaw would care to share a cell with."

Corrigan asked, "Is that what you'd be after calling them milk train robbers, then, insincere outlaws?"

Longarm said, "Too early to tell. They just may have a *motive*. Unless they do, I don't see how they qualify as real outlaws."

Corrigan frowned and pointed out, "It's against the law to be after stopping a train on its tracks and making everbody get off and all!"

Longarm nodded but insisted, "To what end at what profit? Unless the four of them are up to something dumb as a fraternity initiation, there has to be a *motive* none of us have figured, yet!"

He asked directions to the dairy those milk cans had shown up late at.

Corrigan pointed back the way he'd come and explained, "You'd have been after riding past their loading platform because they don't have their sign overlooking where the train would be after stopping. It's towards the

42

town they've aimed their grand sign and all. We yard workers *know* where the place would be."

Longarm allowed that was one on him and remounted to ride back the way he'd come. This time, knowing what he was looking for, he had no trouble spotting the loading platform of Trinidad Butter & Eggs. He reined in, dismounted and tethered Candy to a canopy post to stride on into a scene of some confusion until he figured out what was going on.

The cement floor of the barnlike interior was awash with soapy water as milk cans clattered and banged. The air hung thick and steamy with the smell of hot water, lye soap, and cream. A Mexican hosing down the floor cussed Longarm out of his way as other workers, Mex or Mission Indian men and women, tore around like denizens of a stomped-on ant hill. As he made his way through the confusion toward the front he began to sort out what had to be going on. They'd taken delivery from another milk train earlier that morning and now they were cleaning up after sending their delivery trucks out. It made more sense, as soon as you studied on it, to unload the milk train from the rear of the plant, process the produce as it moved forward, and send it on its way from the front side, facing town and naturally the wagon routes into the same.

The emptied milk cans had to be boiled in swamping basins of first caustic soda, milder soap suds to tame the lye, then hosed out with warm neutral water before they wound up in a big stack, upside down so as to drain. He could see how, like livestock, the owners had marked their own individual cans to be returned. On the far side of the cleaning operation he was just able to see, through rising steam, how others on another line seemed to be tidying up an egg-packing line. He figured the machinery he heard somewhere in the distance might be churning butter. A dairy big enough to supply even a small town was quite

43

an operation. It had that bakery run by Arapaho pals in Denver beat by half.

A tough-looking galoot in bib overalls was suddenly blocking Longarm's path to demand who the hell he thought he was and where the hell he thought he was going.

When Longarm explained he was the law, there to see about the troubles they'd been having with their Friday morning deliveries, the foreman or whatever pouted, "You should have come in the front way. The office is open to the street out front and we try to keep things *clean* back here! You had no call to track through here in those dirty boots!"

Longarm glanced down at the quater inch of soapy water they were both standing in to allow he was sorry as hell about his muddy tracks. Then he strode on to where, sure enough, a sign hung from a steam pipe was shaped like an arrow as it announced, FRONT OFFICE.

Longarm strode on through the rear entrance of the same, braced for more arguments from some crusty son of a bitch who'd beat his suppliers down on the price of milk.

But he saw nobody in the office but a dishwater blond teenager who might have been older than that when you looked at her closer. She was wearing a fresh white linen smock over a darker skirt that showed south of its hem. She looked surprised by the sight of Longarm as well. She asked how he'd gotten in from her rear. He assumed she didn't mean that the way it could be taken and explained, "I came in from the loading dock. Your help out back already told me not to do that again, ma'am. I'd be Deputy U.S. Marshal Custis Long and I'd like a word with the boss about the trouble you all have been having with those Friday morning mystery riders."

She said, "You're talking to the boss. I'd be the Widow Fenton, Ruth Fenton. Everything you see around here is mine, lock stock and barrel since my man went down in the Battle of Trinidad over a dozen years ago."

Longarm gulped and said, "I'm sure sorry to hear about that, ma'am. Might I ask which side your man was fighting for in that big showdown?"

She answered, simply, "Neither. He was trying to deliver the morning milk in the one wagon we started out with when some fool shot him in the head with a .52-caliber buffalo round."

She didn't have to explain, as Longarm followed her drift when she added it had been a closed casket service.

Chapter 6

The not-as-young-as-she-looked Widow Fenton was proud to show Longarm around the operation she'd built from one milk wagon and her own small herd of milch cows on the outskirts of a then-smaller Trinidad. She said she owed a heap to the Colorado Fuel and Iron Company delivering all those immigrant families for her to deliver butter, eggs, and morning milk to. She sounded bitter as she commented on the tendency of Mexicans to drink goat's milk and keep their own blamed chickens underfoot.

She sounded bitter about most everything as she confirmed what Longarm had heard from others about those late early deliveries. When he asked if it had occured to her to pay the going rate for milk just a few hours late she snapped, "I paid for my education. The dairy farmers I've contracted can pay for their own. I agree milk might not spoil that much on a cool spring morning if you bottle it just a little later. But a contract is a contract. Saturday is Saturday and where do you draw the line?"

When he didn't answer she said, "Look, half the milk they deliver to me as fresh was drawn from the udder at three in the afternoon, or better than fourteen hours before it arrived at my loading dock out back. If I were to excuse

even staler produce where could that lead? Why not accept day-old milk as fresh? You think those trash homesteaders would *tell* me milk was going bad if I was too
dumb to sniff it? The contract we agreed on calls for milk
no older than eighteen hours, tops, at the going price. The
fifty-percent penalty for late deliveries is meant to prevent
just that. That long table, yonder, is where my girls pack
the eggs. We used to trust the farmers to candle their
damned eggs for us. Thanks to the the way some betrayed
my trust and upset my customers we candle our eggs ourselves and pay accordingly. Let me show you my new
steam-powered churns, now."

As he followed her through the noisy plant with power
belts flapping over them, Longarm declared, "It ain't for
me to tell you how to run your own beeswax, Miss Ruth,
but didn't some Texas dairyman named Borden lick spoil-
age quite some time ago? And I understand this big dairy
up in the state capital slows things down considerable
with a combination of ammonia pipes and that process of
Professor Pasteur."

She sniffed, "We deal in neither condensed nor pas-
teurized dairy products at Trinidad Butter and Eggs, I'll
have you know! Processing milk *kills* it. Would you have
my customers serving their children *dead milk*?"

She proudly pointed to what looked like pint-sized lo-
comotives going nowhere as they huffed and puffed, explaining, "We churn our butter from *living* milk and sell
buttermilk at cost to the county hospital for sick babies to
settle their little bellies with. We only break even on our
cottage cheese as well. But I've been working on a Colorado version of American cheddar and once we get it to
come out orange and firm instead of mustard green and
runny . . ."

He said, "Miss Ruth, you might as well hear this from
a friend. Some here in town suspect you've taken unfair
advantage of them milk train whatevers. I can see why
you find it fair to pay less for late delivery. I can see how

it would complicate your bookkeeping if you were to pass the savings on to your customers one delivery out of the week. So up front with the cards on the table, how much in exact figures have you come out ahead three weekends in a row?"

He expected her to shilly shally. She answered right out, "Around six hundred dollars more than usual. You have to understand the ten or twelve hundred a day I usually take in is *gross* profit, not *net*. By the time I pay out my overhead I bank a little better than a hundred a week and if you think that's more than I deserve, go buy your own damned cow!"

Longarm laughed and said, "I'm sure you're worth every penny if you'll allow a hundred a week in honest earnings is one thing, whilst a hundred a *day* for a rider risking ten or more years at hard would be another."

She said she didn't understand.

He said, "The figures don't add up against you, Miss Ruth. Tomfoolery to avoid paying out six hundred dollars would call for you and four outlaws splitting a mighty modest prize. Less than two hundred apiece if it was a fair split and even dumber on their part if you kept as much as two hundred for your ownself."

She sniffed like a society lady noticing fingerprints on her glassware and said, "For heaven's sake, if I had four armed outlaws working for me I'd have them rob one of the banks along Main Street!"

He soberly replied, "I just said that, if not in them exact words. I ain't saying it's right or wrong for you to penalize them homesteaders for the sins of others. I can see where you'd think it fair and I understand the railroad's paying them for their losses and passing the burden on to their insurance company. What I *don't* see is who could be making half enough on the deal to justify the risk. Armed posses have been chasing those four boys with serious intent to do them bodily harm and after that it's only a question of time before somebody, on one side or the other, gets seriously harmed or worse. You keep waving loaded guns around and sooner or later one goes off!"

She asked him if he wanted to see how her hands made her cheese boxes from steamed cottonwood. He said he had to get it on up the road if he meant to crack the case before Friday.

She never asked what he meant to do, come Friday. So he didn't have to lie to her. He was already regretting the fact he'd disclosed those sort of obvious plans to more than one there in Trinidad. For the more he studied on it, the more obvious it seemed that someone there in town had to be behind whatever in blue blazes they were up to. Neither bronco Apache nor border buscaderos fit the consistent description of those four riders, one possibly a Mex given to jackass laughing but at least one of 'em ordering folk off trains in a plain American way.

Mounting up again out back, Longarm considered how he might *change* his stated plans, now that he'd stated 'em, as he crossed the yards to ride up into Nuevo Trinidad, where things got more crowded than quaint.

No two Indian reservations or company towns looked exactly alike. Yet they all bore a family resemblance. Once you knew that look you could always recognize it for what it was, a satisfied snob's notion of what was good enough for lesser beings.

It wasn't as if the identical four-square frame cottages north of the tracks were all that inferior to the older housing of Corazon de Trinidad. Some of the poorer Mex families lived in squalid dirt-floored jacals of brushwood improvised in gaps between more substantial 'dobes that were made, in point of fact, of sun-dried mud. But such humble abodes tended to be punctuated by more substantial frame or baked brick buildings and none of them looked exactly the *same*. Like Topsy, the Corazon de Trinidad had just grown, like something alive, over spaces of time according to human whim, whilst every company cottage for block after block had been built to the same plans and specs with pragmatic board-and-baton sidings and the same tar-papered roofs at the same practical pitch with the same galvanized iron chimney poking through the same place in every tar-papered roof.

You could even judge for yourself where one coal company's corporate housing left off and another began with a vacant lot or more betwixt the uniform rows of identical houses. Each company's carpenters worked to a slightly different but always as practical set of plans and specs. Coal mine owners didn't build cottages quite as nice as you found in a hardrock mining town. Coal miners were paid a third as much as hardrock drill crews for several practical reasons the mine owners found fair enough.

To begin with, gold, silver, or even copper ore was worth way more a ton than soft coal. After that, whilst it was just as dangerous down in a coal mine it took more skill to drill through hard rock than soft coal. A greenhorn only needed guts, determination, and a lot of luck to dig his expected tonnage. So greenhorns off the boat would work for no more than a dollar a day and if they didn't like it they could see if they could make it as a cowhand at the same wages, seeing as they'd learned so much riding and roping in their old countries.

English-speaking Welshmen refused to dig coal for those wages whilst less experienced Irishmen, being as able to speak English, tended to either quit or cause trouble in the coal fields. Bohunks, or Bohemian hardrock miners, could usually manage better-paying jobs in the Rockies. Italians, Poles, and Greeks gravitated to towns such as Ludlow or Trinidad with the current population of Nuevo Trinidad mostly Italians and Greeks with some Irish already moving up in the world as foremen or better because they spoke English and understood the situation.

The street grid northwest of the tracks sat squarer to the cardinal points of the compass and they called the streets avenues, with Arizona Avenue the north-south main thoroughfare as a sort of continuation of Commercial Street to the south. In place of company housing, Arizona Avenue had company stores, saloons, barber shops, and such, each as much like a kid's wooden block as the other.

When he spotted a paper streamer along the front of a storefront that declared it the local headquarters of the American Populist Party he told Candy, "This must be the place," and reined in to dismount, tether her to their hitch rail, and mosey on in.

Not unlike the agricultural Granger Movement and sometimes working with the same, the Populists had aims somewhere left of the Democrats and right of red flag outfits like the Knights of Labor or that newer Western Federation of Mine Workers. He was still surprised to see the Populists operating openly out of a company storefront. Most mine owners considered the incumbent Republican Party followers of Mister Karl Marx.

Since the square frame structure had been built as a store, a counter running wall to wall divided the entry space from whatever they'd once sold from the back. That morning there were typewriters and a small hand-printing press at work in the back with both men and women yelling back and forth as he came in.

They all fell silent as a burly older gent with a bushy head and a beard Karl Marx would have been proud to own came over to the counter to ask Longarm what they could do for him.

Longarm flashed his badge and ID as he explained, "I'm working on those milk train robberies you may have heard tell of. There's been some talk about them being staged to discredit your Republican sheriff with an election coming up. Your turn."

The Populist organizer shook his bushy head and said, "Not us. We don't have anyone running for county office, yet. We're still having enough of a time convincing greenhorns who don't speak English it's their duty to register

51

and vote for *anybody*. But mark my words and watch the dust of a comer called Davis H. Waite. For if we ever have a Populist governor old Davis will be the man. Younger than me with a grander beard and he can talk the horns off a billy goat in basso profundo."

Longarm nodded and said, "Read about him in the *Rocky Mountain News*. They tried to run him out of Pueblo and he didn't run. Says it's time for an eight-hour day, free silver, and that limey income tax. Can't see him getting elected as dog catcher albeit that eight-hour day sounds sort of reasonable."

He started to fish for some smokes, decided it would be impolite not to offer any to the ones in the back and set the thought aside as he went on, "If you all ain't for or against the current sheriff what *are* you up to with your new banner and them posters you seem to be printing in the back?"

The Populist in charge easily replied, "Fair wages, for now. Voters can't think straight about less pressing social issues when they're so worried about where their next meal may be coming from. They call us red flaggers and worse for trying to organize their workers. But what would you call competing mine owners who meet in smoke-filled rooms to fix the price of coal to the public and the wages of those who dig it?"

Longarm said, "Businessmen. Them anti-trust proposals raised most every session by junior congressmen never seem to get off the table. What might you call fair wages for digging coal?"

The Populist said, "What's only *fair*, Dad blast it! We're not out to ruin a good thing for anybody. We're not pushing for a dollar a day with no minimum tonnage, like that radical WFMW. We agree the owners have the right to demand a day's work for a day's pay. But is it fair to offer a man a flat dollar a shift and slave-drive unreasonable sweat out of him? We hold it to be self-evident and only fair there should be some minimum tonnage based on the average man's capacity or else they ought to pay extra by say ten cents a ton once a crew's exceeded its usual quota."

Longarm said, "Sounds fair to me. But I don't own no coal seams and the question before the house is who's been messing with the price of *milk* in these parts."

The would-be labor organizer said he hadn't heard anything about the price of milk going up or down.

Longarm had just said he'd heard as much from others when the plate glass behind him shattered and something about the size of a brick hit the counter he was standing at to bounce off, spinning, closer to his feet.

Longarm was still alive after Shiloh and worse because he thought fast on those feet. So the short fuse of the dynamite bomb was still sputtering as he dropped to one knee to grab and throw as the older man behind the counter was still marveling, "What the fuck . . . ?"

The four lashed-together sticks of sixty-percent Hercules sailed out the same direction it had been thrown from to detonate in mid-air.

Glass tinkled down from shattered windows along Arizona Avenue as the reverberations still echoed back and forth across Nuevo Trinidad. But the more disturbing noises were coming from poor old Candy, tethered out front.

The bit was still in her mouth and the reins still held as she lashed her head in pain whilst she writhed on one side in the dust. As Longarm stepped outside through the shattered front window he could see how some dedicated devil worshipper had stuck nails like cloves in the putty-soft dynamite.

Drawing his .44-40 as he got to the torn and bleeding mare, Longarm told her in a soothing tone, "I'm sorry as hell about this, Candy."

His tone seemed to steady the bewildered critter. She could have felt he was bending over to pet her. He could only hope so as he put the muzzle to that hollow over her eye and blew her brains out.

Chapter 7

Mining towns seemed busy for their size because at least a third of the miners were off duty and awake at all hours. So by the time half a dozen roundsmen showed up with that fat detective Longarm had talked to earlier, a considerable crowd had gathered, muttering the same dark suspicions in more than one lingo. Las Animas Amalgamated Mines came out much the same in Italian, Greek, or brogue.

The fat detective's name was Caruso, even though he talked natural. He had his notebook out. But Longarm had to allow he'd had his fool back to all that glass when a person or persons unknown had heaved a nail bomb through it.

The Populist organizer, who'd been facing the street from behind the counter, could offer no more than somebody he'd taken for a drunken cowboy streaking past at full gallop on a bay mount. When Longarm asked if it could have been a Cavalry bay the older man looked away and said he'd been too young for the war.

Caruso asked if Longarm was thinking what he was thinking about nondescript bay mounts. Longarm shrugged and said, "No law saying those four riders who keep stopping the milk train are the only ones allowed to bid on those surplus cavalry nags the remount service keeps dumping on the market and this *is* a political set up. On the other hand, we still don't know why they've been stopping that milk train. Why do they have to have a sensible motive to bomb somebody else?"

Caruso surprised Longarm some more by observing, "Remount sells fairly sudden stock as it gets to be eight years old. Still legged-up and bigger than cow or Indian ponies. You don't need a cutting horse or roper when all you want from your mount is better than average speed and tracing an army bay back to the original bidder can be a bother. Half the livery nags across the land wear fading U.S. brands, bless their uniform hides!"

He stepped back out on the walk to canvas the crowd for any others who might have gotten a better look at that galloping bay. A gent who'd been waiting for a haircut across the way was able to establish the rider had torn downhill toward the rail yards instead of out of town the other way, where he might have left a son-of-a-bitching *trail*. That witness was able to put a gray hat with its crown telescoped Colorado style on the bomb-throwing bastard on the bay.

Caruso ordered four of his followers to canvas both sides of Arizona down to the railroad yards and beyond. One of the Populist Party men in the back knew where Longarm could hire a moving man with a mule and a low-slung dray. Others in the crowd were sports about helping Longarm get the dead cordovan mare aboard. He rinsed Candy's fresh blood off his own saddle and bridle with the help of a pump-fed watering trough just down the way before he and the moving man hauled poor old Candy back to her Mexican owner down in the Corazon de Trinidad.

The old Mex was a good sport about it when they deposited what was left of Candy in his dooryard. He allowed she'd led a full life, died in a good cause and felt

Longarm's deposit along with what he could get from the knackers for her would do him.

He waited until Longarm had paid off the moving man and sent him on his way before he looked around as if they might not be alone and told Longarm, "I can recruit some bravos for to watch your back, *El Brazo Largo*. Is most *claro* who was trying for to kill you with that *bomba*, no?"

Longarm said, "No. They were more likely after the radical laborites I was jawing with and we're pretty far north of the border to be jawing about what *Los Rurales* call this child."

The Mexican said, "We are not *that* far and you are not the only lawman with the long arm, if you wish for to call those gray hats riding for El Presidente Diaz the *law*. Is it not true they have posted a handsome bounty on the head of *El Brazo Largo*, dead or alive? Let us help you, for *La Causa de Mejico Libre!*"

Longarm handed the older man a smoke and lit it for him as he insisted he didn't suspect any Mexican bounty hunters to begin with and worked a lot better alone in any case.

He said, "Just before he commenced to lose his touch, poor old James Butler Hickok whirled 'round in a gunfight to shoot his own deputy. They say he never got over it and it slowed him down as it likkered him up. So I like to know there's nobody on my side when *I* get into such situations."

"They will kill you. No man should stand alone against *Los Rurales!*" the Mex livery man insisted. But he didn't grab hold and hang on as Longarm allowed he had other beeswax to tend before noon.

He dropped off the saddle and bridle at his hotel and strode on.

The Las Animas Amalgamated Mines Incorporated had their office in town near Main and Chestnut. A not bad-looking receptionist showed him into an office much like

56

Billy Vail's oak paneled inner sanctum up in Denver, save for smelling nicer. The white-haired Farnsworth T. Binkle presiding behind a whole lot of desk told Longarm to have a seat as he offered him a havana perfecto. As in the case at Trinidad Butter and Eggs, Longarm found he'd come braced for an argument nobody wanted to have with him.

Binkle had already heard about the bombing. By that time everyone in Trinidad on either side of the river and railroad tracks had heard about the bombing. Farnsworth T. Binkle said it was awful. Longarm filled the mining man in on some details he hadn't heard and casually added how odd he'd thought it was to find a radical labor organization headquartered in a storefront they'd rented from Las Animas Amalgamated Mines.

As Longarm got the swell cigar going on his own side of the desk his smiling host explained, "You can catch more flies with honey than you can with vinegar, Deputy Long. Or should I say a wise man keeps friends at a cool distance and hugs his enemies close? The Populists needed some place in town to set up shop. We weren't about to keep them out of town and that storefront nobody else wanted to hire right now rents for fifty dollars a month. Who would you *have* us rent it to, the fucking WFMW or the Knights of Labor?"

Longarm blew a thoughtful smoke ring and said, "I follow your drift. The Populists make speeches whilst the WFMW calls strikes and the Knights of Labor, like the Molly Maguires they've about replaced, sabotage and worse. Meanwhile, as is the case with the Granger Movement in the corn belt further east, the marginally radical Populists figure on cutting into the more traditional votes of the Democrats you're more worried about!"

Binkle beamed and said, "You do understand current Colorado political realities. We who own or manage the mines, railroads, and more traditional businesses out this way naturally vote the right way, but we don't have the

57

numbers we need with the infernal cattlemen and all their cowboys tending to vote all wrong."

He chewed his own cigar and growled, "After President Hayes ended the last Reconstruction regulations and restored the Texas Rangers, the ungrateful ruffians! The Mexicans don't like either the Democrats or the Republicans to register with either, bless their ignorant asses, so the key votes here in Las Animas County, come November, are up for grabs in Nuevo Trinidad, with those fucking Irishmen out to register every Greek and Dago as a Democrat!"

"Unless somebody can get them to vote Populist," nodded Longarm.

That had been a statement rather than a question. But Farnsworth T. Binkle answered, "Damned A. So tell me why anyone riding for us or any of the other members of our management clique want to put the Populists out of business with a bomb?"

Longarm said, "No offense, but you sound more reasonable than some big shots in these parts and I keep hearing about this Davis H. Waite the Populists propose to run for higher office one of these days."

The pragmatic Binkle shrugged and said, "Not in this century, at the rate their movement's growing, and even if by some miracle they *do* put one of their own in the governor's mansion, what will that mean?"

Longarm suggested, "Eight-hour days, free silver, and an income tax?"

Binkle snorted, "A bearded radical transformed to a sensible conservative by the time they swear him in. You mark my words and if Davis H. Waite is ever elected to a position of any authority his utopian followers are in for the usual cold gray dawn. It's one thing to make speeches about political reforms. It's another thing entire to get the leopard to change its spots."

Longarm tried, "What do you think of the notion somebody's out to try for some changes in these parts and is out to discredit your sheriff's department by staging those otherwise loco milk train holdups?"

Farnsworth T. Binkle said he took his breakfast coffee black and his kids were grown up and back east. He suggested, "Why don't you ask the Atcheson Topeka and Santa Fe if they're putting on extra Pinkerton men? Our own Company Police hands made that suggestion shortly after the bullshit started."

Longarm started to say that was a dumb suggestion. But when he studied on it he had to morosely admit, "I thank you a bunch for adding *that* worm to the can I was already staring down at!"

Binkle asked him how much your average railroad dick made. Longarm said, "Almost as much as me and I already said thanks a bunch!"

The smiley-faced Binkle saw him out to the door. It was too late to pester anybody at the railroad depot before they'd have left for their own noon dinners. So he headed back for the Columbian Hotel to see if old Alda was up yet.

Along the way he had an uneasy moment as a buckboard passed with a familiar cordovan carcass half-hidden by a bloodstained tarp. Longarm stopped and saluted, feeling awkward but not knowing what else to do or say as poor old Candy passed on her way to the knackers, where they'd salvage her hide, boil her hooves for glue, then grind her flesh for dog food and her bones for rose gardens. That was how you wound up when you were a horse. Longarm wasn't certain it was unfair. He'd read how one of those New Zealand Maori had found it shocking the English soldiers killed folk they had no intention of *eating* and where would the world be if even dead *critters* rated graveyard space?

It still seemed a shame, when you'd known the critter well enough to call it by name, though.

Back at the hotel he found Alda not only up, but having dinner, room service, up in her suite with a smirky

59

dude she introduced as a Wilfred Rockwell from Chicago. They were both fully dressed and when Longarm said he might try the Harvey House, himself, Alda told him not to be a goof. So he drew up another chair, idly wondering what the balding skinny dude from Chicago had made of that exchange. When another waiter appeared as if by magic Alda waved an airy hand at the window to explain she'd seen him coming back from wherever and pulled that magic cord by the time he'd made it to the lobby entrance.

Then she naturally wanted to know where he'd been.

Longarm told their waiter he'd have whatever the dude from Chicago had just about finished and sent him on his way before he even tried to bring the two insurance folk up to date on his busy morning.

Alda gasped he could have been killed. Old Wilfred asked what it added up to. Longarm said, "It don't add up to anything sensible at all. I've yet to talk to this section of the AT&SFRR yet. Have either of you?"

Wilfred Rockwell said, "About the time you would have been at Trinidad Butter and Eggs. They agreed to a five-hundred-dollar settlement for each holdup or fifteen hundred all together. In exchange they agreed to try a little harder. They're putting railroad police who don't normally guard a milk train aboard, what else, their milk train."

Longarm said, "That was one of the things I meant to take up with 'em. As I understand from jawing with railroad men in the caboose on many a long haul, no railroad makes money on passenger service or short-haul day freight. They provide such services to keep the voting public happy and make their real profits hauling serious distances as the pennies per mile add up."

Rockwell grimaced and said, "I was just told the same, up along the tracks. They'd as soon drop that unprofitable milk train as fight for the right to haul milk and other fresh produce at cost. But in its infinite wisdom Congress granted all these western railroad rights of way with strings attached. One string being no railroad that wants to go on rolling makes anybody mad enough to affect *election* outcomes!"

The waiter came in with Longarm's order. That was when he found out old Wilfred Rockwell was a fucking freak who ate *creamed spinach* with his *fish* on a fucking *Tuesday*!

But Longarm had to be a sport unless he aimed to insult the harmless little dude and, what the hell, the coffee wasn't bad.

As he picked at his entree whilst they had their own coffee with that *blanc-mange* Alda favored, the conversation drifted back to how much the railroad would have to pay those extra armed guards. When Longarm said they'd likely draw twenty or more a week Rockwell whistled and suggested that as a motive, elaborating, "Suppose four out-of-work Pinkerton men with time on their hands and horses at their disposal . . ."

Longarm started to say they were talking mighty high risk for mighty modest profits. But as he remembered Rockford was used to prices back Chicago way, where sides of beef went for way less than many a poker game pot in mining country, he had to remind himself how easy it was, out this way, to lose track of one's dollars and *sense*.

In a US of A where the average working stiff raised his kids on a dollar a day or less it was easy to be led astray by the bodacious high living of plutocrats like Silver Dollar Tabor, said to pay more than two hundred dollars for a *nightshirt* as he kept a wife he was tired of in one forty thousand dollar Denver brownstone while he kept his young mistress in another he'd paid more for. But when you got down to the fine print, where men worked nine-hour shifts for three dollars, even down in gold mines, the notion of a railroading emergency staged

61

so a pal might get a good job didn't sound all that impossible.

Longarm passed on Alda's offer of *blanc-mange*, without ever saying he thought it tasted like library paste with a teaspoon of sugar stirred in. He wasn't paying attention as Rockwell made mention of getting on back to Chicago, until the squirt asked Alda when she'd be headed back up to Denver.

Alda sounded innocent enough as she casually said something about not wanting to get into Denver during the early evening crush. The Chicago boy missed the look that passed betwixt her and Longarm as she allowed she might stay over in Trinidad another night.

Chapter 8

Early railroaders had learned back in the thirties about the awful things that could happen when you had tons of steam-driven steel moving fast as a brisk walk along tracks nobody was watching like a hawk. Thanks to the Morse telegraph, trains could be, and therefore were, passed like relay batons from one discreetly managed section to the next, with each section of single track divided into blocks no more than one train was supposed to move along at the same time. The section security chief Longarm talked to that afternoon, up by the depot both railroads shared, was an affable but pragmatic old railroader who cheerfully admitted a hand in the famous shoot-out with the D&RGRR in the Royal Gorge and a couple of lesser known shoot-outs since. But he didn't care for a shoot-out with pranksters who hadn't purloined a lump of coal from any train *he* gave a shake about.

He said, "Mex kids along the line throw rocks at the tender in hopes the fireman might throw coal back at them. I've ordered 'em not to. I've ordered our milk train crews not to get into a gunfight over milk or even eggs unless those mystery riders get *personal*!"

"What about butter?" asked Longarm, dryly.

The Santa Fe security expert said, "Them small holders

don't churn their own butter. I understand the Widow Fenton don't trust them to candle their own eggs. My point is that we're talking fresh but modestly priced produce, not the wool, hides, or bulk coal we make our *money* moving. Makes more sense to go along with their foolery, deliver the produce an hour or so late and to hell with it."

Longarm said, "I understand your line has had to make up the losses of those local dairy farmers?"

The railroad gun shrugged and said, "That's what insurance premiums pay for. Just had words about that with this jasper from Chicago. He's after us to deliver the morning milk under armed guard. I told him we'd study on it. I did put his suggestions on the wire to our company headquarters. Banana oil costs nothing. They'll study on it some. Then they'll agree it's safer and cheaper to just pick up the late-charge slack for our local custom and pass the costs on to our insurance underwriters."

"Ain't they likely to raise your premiums if you don't even try to get all that milk to town on time?"

The railroad gun shrugged and replied, "They can try. They ain't the only insurance underwriters covering one hell of a railroad operation. We've built far west as Deming, New Mexico, with a view to pushing on all the way to Pueblo de Los Angeles, with depots, crews, and rolling stock on back to Kansas covered by insurance."

He let that sink in before he smugly added, "You'd risk the premiums covering the length of this man's railroad by jacking up the premiums of this one section?"

Longarm said, "You sure seem to have 'em by the short hairs and I have to admit I'd give your crews the same advice. Makes no sense to risk a *fistfight* when nobody's even asking for your pocket jingle."

Then, seeing they'd agreed on that, he asked, "So what do you reckon those daring milk train robbers are really after?"

The older world-weary railroad gun mused, "Asshole fun is all I can come up with. I know everyone's agreed they seem grown men. A big kid with his beardless chin masked might pass for a grown man. A grown man acting like an asshole kid ain't that unusual. Some sort of fraternity initiation works for me."

"Three Saturday morns in a row?" asked Longarm.

The older and apparently less concerned security man replied, "I'm open to other suggestions. I just work here. Nobody tells me nothing. If I knew who they were and why they were doing it I'd ask them to stop. We both know that if they don't stop their luck is bound to run out and we can go on down to Firehouse Number One and just *ask* them what in blue blazes they thought they were doing."

Longarm said, "My orders are to crowd 'em closer. I'm still working on the logistics, but who would I have to clear it with if I wanted to sneak myself aboard next Friday's milk train with my saddlegun and say sixteen hands of Trakehner or Thoroughbred?"

The railroad gun said, "You've talked to him. I'll put out the word. If I had my druthers I'd chase the assholes with a Cavalry Trakehner. Thoroughbred can overtake anything on flat range. But the quartet who've been stopping our milk trains for whatever reason have ridden hard for the higher and rougher range to the west, all three times, unless we've missed something."

As he left Longarm was already wondering where he'd be able to come by enough horses for the job.

By all accounts the four ponies he meant to chase were army bays at best or, even better for the chaser, bay cow ponies. And despite a lot of Noble Savage twaddle, sold-off army mounts tended to be getting on in years and short of wind whilst, as Mister Lo the poor Indian kept finding out the hard way, no Indian pony or its close cousin, the cow pony, was about to outdistance a serious no-bullshit *horse*.

Cavalry officers were allowed to ride personal stock and often bought pricey imported Hanover, Orlov, Thoroughbred, or Trakehner cavalry stock. The Army Remount Service chose more by configuration than bloodlines on the notion that a horse that came up to its standards had to be by definition a good horse.

Most army mounts were that breed of uncertain ancestry but definite lines known as the American Saddle Breed, two hands or a good eight inches taller at the shoulder than the chunkier Indian or cow pony and hence a mount starting out with longer legs and a greater stride. Many agile if slower cow ponies had spines a vertebra or more shorter if they had Hispano-Moorish "Barb" in them.

The Army Remount Service chose otherwise uniform gray horses for the musicians of the regimental bands to ride. Otherwise they tried for the same shade of chestnut bay most natural to the cooler-blooded and taller European breeds, with the Thoroughbred having a tad more Arab blood and hence more fire, without losing its size advantage. Race horses raced so well because they combined all that was fast in a horse.

Cowboys as well as Indians were inclined to stretch the marginal edge of the so-called Mustang heritage of their fourteen-hand ponies. They were in fact more agile and could turn tighter than most cavalry mounts. After that the cavalry trooper standing in his stirrups and slashing down from eight more inches of horse was nobody to be messed with lightly and after that the bigger grain-fed cavalry stock could chase the runty grass-fed Indian pony down most every time. Few Indians or outlaws on grass-fed cow ponies could hope to stay out ahead of the US Cav's thirty-mile-a-day etapes. The Army Remount Service managed such standards by selling off eight year olds, still in their prime, albeit about in the shape of a healthy thirty-year-old athlete.

So those outlaws could be mounted on better than average stock a *really* good horse should be able to overtake. The next question before the house was what one man on one horse was supposed to do when he caught up with the four of them.

But Saturday morn lay over more than eighty hours out ahead and thanks to the eating habits of Wilfred Rockwell, Longarm was hungry as a bitch wolf. So, whistling *Farther Along* he mosied on to the neary Harvey House to wrap himself around some damn *dinner!*

With no train in the station he naturally found the famous Harvey Gals at betwixt trains chores such as mopping the floor or wiping off the tables. They seemed confused by his barging in and sitting down as if he thought he was expecting to be fed.

Nobody came near him. All six Harvey gals on duty huddled by the kitchen door with more than one shooting nervous glances his way. All wore the same company uniform, a spotless white apron over a dress the color of his Stetson. They had their hair pinned up in the same buns. Fred Harvey hired young single women who were supposed to stay single as long as they were working for him. Needless to say he didn't hire fat nor ugly gals, albeit he shot for wholesome-pretty rather than head-turning trouble.

Once they'd established he wasn't going to just go away, a bolder one came over to tell him they hadn't been fixing to serve again until the eastbound three-fifteen pulled in out back.

Longarm said, "I can't wait that long, ma'am. I was invited to dinner over at the Columbian and they stuck me with spinach and fish. Carp, I suspect. I never ate much of it and I passed entire on the *blanc-mange* dessert!"

She dimpled down at him and said, "Oh, you poor thing! I'll see what I can rustle up in the kitchen if you'll be a sport about the menu. Our cooks are creatures of habit who throw things when they get upset."

Longarm laughed, said he'd settle for anything that didn't bite back and she trilled her way into the kitchen to see what they had on hand. The others went back to work, getting ready for the three-fifteen as if he wasn't there. That was the secret of the Harvey operation. Not having their own dining cars, the AT&SFRR made three meal stops a day where their passengers were required to know what they wanted as they got off, eat it soon as it was served and get back on the damned train. So as in the case of army recruits, the Harvey girls had to know how to hurry up and wait, serving fairly good grub at moderate price and breakneck speed. They were famous for serving coffee cool enough to drink at once with the sugar and cream customers might order already stirred in. Their blue plate specials were served with the roast beef already cut into bite-sized chunks, and your bread or rolls came already buttered. Harvey's wholesome no-bullshit service had become so popular along the route of the AT&SFRR that he'd started some regular restaurants in some towns along the way, where customers got to take more time and butter their own bread if they had a mind to. Such jewels in his corporate crown were staffed by more experienced Harvey gals who'd managed to build some seniority whilst staying out of trouble. Getting married up or having a boyfriend the management noticed got a Harvey gal in trouble.

The one who'd taken pity on him returned with a tray worth every penny of the fifty cents she said he owed her, up front. As if worried a train whistle would snatch him away, she'd loaded the tray with a partitioned blue plate, his apple pie with rat trap cheese dessert and a mug of black coffee. When he said, "Lord love you, I was afraid you'd put cream and sugar in this coffee when you ran off before I could tell you not to!"

She said, "I remembered you took your coffee black. You are the one they call Longarm, aren't you?"

He glanced up from the meat loaf, mashed potatoes, and buttered beans he'd been admiring to meet the gaze of her elfin eyes of sea green. The eyes were the part that confounded him. For a man might lose track of auburn hair swept up the same as any other Harvey gal's and all fine figures looked much the same with clothes on. But whilst a pretty face was a pretty face he was sure he'd remember those green eyes better if he'd ever gazed into them doing anything at all serious to their owner.

As if she could read his mind the Harvey gal said, "I didn't think you remembered me."

"I was just now wondering about that very thing," Longarm lied, adding with a confiding smile, "I was afraid you'd suspect I was trying to get fresh if I asked you if I hadn't seen you someplace before. No offense, but the way all you ladies dress the same . . ."

"I was wearing this same company uniform in Topeka!" she flared before she turned to flounce away.

Longarm thought about the few times he'd been as far east as Topeka, knew for certain he'd never even kissed a green-eyed Harvey gal there, and dug in to the sort of skimpy but mighty tasty snack she'd served him. She never came back from the kitchen before he'd not only finished but lingered over his empty coffee mug with a luxurious three-for-a-nickel smoke a spell.

But he never finished his smoke at the table. For, seeing she seemed to be hiding in the kitchen on purpose, Longarm left a handsome quarter tip by his polished off plate and got up from the table as off in the distance he heard another Harvey gal giggle.

He was still wondering where in thunder he'd seen such a pretty gal who'd made so little impression on him as he covered the other bases he knew Billy Vail expected him to.

Having heard the established Republican and radical Populist sides he ambled along Main to scout up the Democrats of Trinidad. They had a big sign over their own store front, in English, Spanish, Italian, and Greek, if he was right about those odd letters.

Inside a florid Irish-American with jet black hair tried to get Longarm to register to vote and when that didn't work he was a sport about it, took him in a back office where he just happened to have a fifth of Canadian in his rolltop desk, and sat them both down for a confidential chat.

Longarm left forty-five minutes later walking sort of funny and not knowing a blamed thing he hadn't known before. So after wasting more time at the land office in a vain attempt to find any nester threatened with eviction if he didn't get his milk to market on time, Longarm headed back to the hotel to see if Alda had gotten rid of old Wilfred yet.

She had, and she'd changed back into that kimono whilst waiting for him. So, seeing it was getting late for more investigating and still too early to order anything else from room service, they shucked and jumped in bed for some daylight slap and tickle.

"Oh, my God, I keep forgetting how good that feels!" Alda sobbed as he mounted her with two pillows under her shapely bare rump.

He just kept humping with neither argument nor agreement. For everyone who'd ever done so on more than one occasion knew Dame Nature allowed a poor mortal to set such feelings aside for hours at a time lest the human race fuck itself to death whilst never getting another thing done.

But as she embraced his hot heaving flesh with all four limbs and her warm wet innards it did indeed seem as if nothing else on earth mattered next to getting it even deeper in her delicious ring-dang-doo and then, just as he was fixing to come and trying to hold back for just one more teasing stroke, the whole bed rose from the floor and their love nest roared around them like the core of a lightning flash for what seemed forever. Then the bed thudded to the floor to shake them up harder as they stared at one another in wonder through a haze of plaster dust and the head-splitting reek of nitroglycerine!

"My God! What was that?" Alda gasped as Longarm

70

rolled off her to grab for his jeans on the floor and gunbelt on the bedpost. When he answered tersely, "Dynamite bomb!" she asked, "Are you serious? How come we're both alive if that was a bomb just now?"

He hauled on his jeans and rose, gun in hand, as he said, "Stay put. It was next door, in the room they expected to find me in just now!"

Chapter 9

They seemed to be having a late blizzard out in the hall until Longarm saw what looked like snow was goose-down swirling out the blown open door of his hired room. The draft, swirling fluffy white mattress-stuffing out to the hallway, was coming from the shattered windows on the far side. He made it inside, to stare in wonder at the mess a dynamite bomb made of a feather bed, before he was joined there by the house dick, two bell hops, and desk clerk from downstairs.

The house dick blinked at Longarm to demand, "You're still alive? How come? They blew you out of your boots and tore your shirt off you and I don't see a scratch on what's left!"

"Just lucky, I reckon," Longarm modestly replied as he moved over to inspect the saddle the bastards had blown off the footrail of the torn up bed. As he hunkered down he saw there weren't enough new scuff marks to stew about. Army saddles were made of stout triple-tanned steer hide.

As long as he was down there he got a fresh work shirt out of his saddle bag to put on as he rose, holstering his sixgun to button up. He was just as glad nobody asked him where his boots or hat might be.

The hotel staff was still bemoaning the damage the nails stuck on all that dynamite had done to the plaster walls and tin ceiling when they were joined by town law from that handy Firehouse Number One up Commercial Street. The fat Detective Caruso said he'd suspected Longarm might be on hand when he'd heard yet another muffled dynamite blast. Glancing at the flooring one could now see through what had been the center of that bed, Caruso asked, "Where the hell were you when it went off and are we still wondering who the target was, Uncle Sam?"

Longarm said, "They were after this child, both times. I wish some outlaws weren't so noisy."

Caruso pointed with his double chin at the nail-gouged walls as far as to either side of the shattered window as he insisted, "Anyone can see they were *after* you, dammit! How did they just miss *killing* you? I can't see a square foot of floor space you could have occupied without taking a whirling nail or more at waist level or lower!"

Longarm said, "I was flat on my gut when the bomb went off," and this was the pure truth when you studied on it.

Caruso looked at the blown apart bed, started to say something dumb, and brightened to say, "Right, you hit the floor as they kicked open the door to lob the bomb in on you and you were still mighty lucky their infernal device wound up in bed instead of on the rug with you!"

Turning to one of the local lawmen with him, the detective said, "He moves fast as hell for a man his size! Snatched up the bomb they'd thrown earlier to throw it right back at them!"

Then he huddled with the hotel help and his notebook in hopes one or more could offer him another description. Longarm drifted out in the hall and nobody asked where he was going. So he didn't have to fib about needing to take a piss when that nail bomb couldn't have done all that much to his adjoining bath.

73

Alda Grey was standing in her own open doorway, fully dressed and looking as if butter wouldn't melt in her mouth as she asked him, for the benefit of other guests in the crowded hallway, "What happened, ah, Deputy Long, right?"

He said, "At your service, ma'am," and followed her on in. She shut the door. So he was free to sit on her less messed-up bed and haul on his socks and boots as he told her, "They've been following me some time with a second nail bomb they whipped up after the first one failed. Had they started with two, things might have been noisier some other places I was this afternoon."

She handed him his jacket as he rose, deciding, "On the other hand they may have aimed to be sure I was alone. I'll ask 'em when I catch 'em. In the meanwhile I owe my life to your pretty little ring-dang-doo and once things simmer down some more around here . . ."

She turned away to softly murmur, "Custis, I'll be boarding the night train to Denver before things are liable to quiet down that much around here."

He took his Stetson from its door hook and put it on as he soberly replied, "Do tell? I was hoping you might want to catch your train home tomorrow, or mayhaps ride back to Denver with me next weekend?"

She said, "After the gloating grin Wilfred Rockwell shot at me as I was seeing him off, earlier? Nobody gossips dirtier than a man a girl's turned down and I'd heard about you and the ladies when I started up with you on the train coming down!"

He grinned sheepishly and said, "They say it pays to advertise, but them stories about me and Miss Sarah Bernhardt, the national treasure of France, ain't true. We never got past cordial whilst I bodyguarded her that time for our State Department."

Alda smiled dirty and said, "Pooh, I was just going to ask you if you laid her in that coffin they say she sleeps in."

He said, "I never and she don't. Leastways, I never saw no coffins in the private railroad car she toured in, out our way. What if you just caught an early morning train up to Denver, honey?"

She sighed and said, "It's over, darling. As a man of the world you have to know it's best to just get up and leave before the champagne goes flat and maybe, sometime, when you get back to Denver . . ."

Someone was calling for him out in the hall. He squared the brim of his Stetson and said, "*Sometime* sounds better than *forever* and I got to see what they want."

So they parted friendly as ships passing in the night and with any luck he wouldn't see her again before she left town.

A roundsman he met in the hallway told Longarm Detective Caruso was asking for him. Longarm rejoined the crowd in this bomb-shattered room next door to find Caruso had been joined by a reporter from the *Trinidad Chronicle News* who marveled, notebook in hand, at Longarm's miraculous escape. Detective Caruso proved he knew his onions and Longarm decided to like the fat rascal better when Caruso took in the Stetson, denim jacket and army boots with a knowing look and never said a word.

The reporter had already covered the bomb blast up on Arizona Avenue and, not being bound by rules of evidence, was off and running with that fuzzy description of a cuss dressed cow on a bay mount.

He said, "This last nail bomb must have been thrown in here by the same bunch and we know those milk train robbers were described as cowhands on bay horses. So we know . . ."

"We don't know toad squat!" Longarm cut in, sternly pointing out, "To begin with this is cow country. Riders wearing English fox-hunting pinks would be unusual riders for these parts. Range riders ain't. After that you get more horses with bay hides than horses of another color. Anybody could be throwing bombs at me. Nobody's thrown bomb one at any milk train. Slow down and look before you leap!"

The reporter demanded, "If those milk train mystery riders aren't the ones after you, who's after you?"

To which Longarm could only reply, "If I knew I'd arrest him. I just ain't ready to say who's out to kill me, albeit it sure looks like he, she, or it ain't out to kill *you*. Whoever may be behind that milk train mystery may not want to risk my getting warm, albeit nobody's tried to kill any other lawmen down this way. It's as likely some personal enemy, knowing I was down this way, hopes to razzle dazzle my pals by making it look as if I was killed by another bunch entire."

Caruso nodded and said, "I wish I had a dollar for every crook I put away who's sworn to get me once he got out. Most of them have seen, by the time they're out, they'd be suspected if anything happened to me."

The reporter brightened and decided, "Sure! Some scoundrel Longarm, here, sent to prison somewhere else is out to frame our home-grown wild bunch with infernal devices!"

The two lawmen exchanged weary looks. Longarm said, "I forgot to tell you the Czar of All the Russians may have secret agents after me because I once checked this book by Mister Tolstoy out of the Denver Public Library and forgot to bring it back."

The reporter started to put that down, snorted in disbelief, and said Longarm was just out to green him.

Then some more local big shots showed up and Longarm let Caruso do the talking as he took the room clerk from downstairs to one side and asked if their insurance was likely to cover the damage.

When the hotel man said he thought so Longarm told him he'd be checking out. The room clerk was too polite to look relieved. But he didn't argue.

So along about sunset things had simmered down to where Longarm felt free to tote his saddle to the nearby older, less expensive but good enough Trinidad House.

He hired a corner room overlooking Commercial Street and stepped out on the balcony for a thoughtful smoke as the scene below got darker and more lively. The cast-iron front had New Orleans–style iron balconies. Likely for the same reasons. The so-called French Quarter of New Orleans was built Spanish style because Spain had owned Louisiana longer than France had. Louisiana folk, like everybody else, seemed to think French sounded fancier.

Had he still been at the fancier Columbian with Alda he'd have already ordered a room service supper off that posh French menu. He was still a tad keyed up but commencing to feel empty again and that reminded him.

He knew better, even as he locked up and wedged a match stem under the bottom hinge of his hotel door as a simple but effective burglar alarm. Harvey gals lived in company dorms under the watchful eyes of chaperones with their room and board making up for the less than twenty dollars a month they made before tips. So far, a thousand or more Harvey gals had married up to refine some western towns a mite. But they'd been laid off with Fred Harvey's congratulations and just plain fired whenever he heard they'd as much as gone dancing with a customer. So a man making a play for a Harvey gal was as optimistic as a man who wrote love letters to famous opera singers who didn't read English.

But he had to eat some damned where and it bothered him when he just couldn't place a pretty face who knew he took his coffee black. They *paid* him to remember faces better than that.

Paying more attention to the time, this time, Longarm ambled into the Harvey House just as a westbound night train was pulling out. So the gals were still clearing the tables and this time, when he sat down, one of them handed him a menu.

77

He ordered a more substantial steak with home fries and a side order of pork and beans with his black coffee and chocolate layer cake, asking her not to let the kitchen help carve his steak because he didn't have a train to catch.

She took his order to the kitchen. He was neither surprised nor at all disappointed when that green-eyed Harvey gal who seemed to know him brought the tray from the same to his table. As she served him she said, "We heard about that bomb at your hotel. What makes you so popular? They were trying to kill you that night in Topeka and it scared me out of a year's growth!"

Longarm laughed with relief as things suddenly fell in place. He asked her, "Was that *you* behind the counter, summer before last, when I tried to treat a prisoner I was transporting to a warm meal and his pals tried to take him back from me?"

She said, "It was. I was on the floor behind the counter while most of the shooting was going on. So all I know about all that noise was that the place looked like the last act of Hamlet, with bodies all over the place, by the time those policemen told us it was safe to get up. By that time you were riding away with your prisoner in that ambulance wagon, so I never got to thank you for the handsome tip."

He said, "I'm glad I left one. Later on, thinking back, I wasn't sure I'd paid before we'd gone. He died at the hospital in the wee small hours but we had to try and it served him right for having such trigger-happy friends. What time do you get off at *this* Harvey House, Miss . . . ?"

"Gross. Judy Gross. I'm on from noon to midnight and I need this job. But I appreciate the thought . . . Longarm?"

He said, "My friends call me Custis, whether I walk them home or not. I was just talking to a newspaper reporter inclined to doll me all up in fringed buckskins and

78

war paint. But if the truth be known I'm only this old West-by-God Virginia boy, just trying to do my job."

She laughed and said, "My ears are still ringing from that job you did on those five gunslicks who started out with the drop on you in Topeka, you modest thing. But enjoy, lest a certain snip who works here report us to management as secret lovers!"

She turned away before he could come up with a clever reply. He knew he'd have one later that evening. That was the trouble with knowing just what to say after it was too late to say it.

He dug in to the plain but wholesome grub Fred Harvey served by way of waitresses you weren't allowed to mess with. The limey spoilsport was right, of course. Out west where men were men and the women were harder to come by you could run a restaurant or you could run a dance hall. You couldn't run a place that tried to be both, and Harvey's no-romance policy no doubt cut down a heap on fistfights or worse.

Judy Gross never came over to even part friendly as Longarm shoved an empty dessert plate away and drank the last of his coffee. He suspected he knew why. That prim-lipped brunette who kept sneaking glances at him from where she was stationed at one end of the counter figured to be the snitch Judy was worried about.

Longarm left another handsome tip and got up to just quit whilst all ahead. No grown man asked a pal to risk losing a good job just so's he could see if she had auburn hair all over. He'd long since resigned himself to the simple fact there was just no way any one man was going to get to lay every pretty gal on earth and, when you studied on it, that thought wasn't all that depressing. For it meant no matter where any man might wander, if he lived to be a hundred, he was never going to run out of pretty gals to try for.

He considered hunting for outlaws in the local saloons. But it had been a long day and he meant to get an early start on the next one. So, seeing it was near the end of May and the June issues of some publications he admired were on the stands he turned in before nine, read the *Police Gazette* front page to last and waded through a couple of articles with might big words in the *Scientific American* before he trimmed his lamp and rolled over to catch some shut-eye.

He'd just noticed for the first time how there was a whole town of Trinidad in a sort of basement, or mayhaps coal mine, under the officious town you saw on the surface, when somebody somewhere seemed to be banging on a big base drum. He thought at first it was one of those gnomes spitting and whittling over on that pile of diamonds. Then he figured it was somebody knocking on a hotel door. So he woke up and, sure enough, the knocking was still going on, and it had to be after midnight.

Chapter 10

It was the hall porter. They'd sent him up to tell Longarm
two gals wanted to talk to him in the lobby. The porter
agreed it was well after midnight, said he didn't know
what the gals downstairs wanted, and added they were
dressed and acted like ladies of quality. So Longarm put
on a fresh shirt and his three piece suit to go on down
and see for himself.

The porter led him to a far corner where Judy Gross
and an older gal with redder hair were seated in the shade
of that odd variety of paper frond palm tree that only grew
in hotel lobbies.

As he got closer in the tricky light he saw the redhead
had been prettier than Judy a few summers back. They
were about even, now. Judy introduced the older gal as
the chaperone from her company dorm, a Miss Elsbeth
Ferguson. She said it was all right to call her Miss Beth
and they both sat down again.

Longarm stayed on his feet as he asked them to what
he owed such an honor at such an hour. Beth Ferguson
nodded at Judy as if giving her the go ahead. Judy said,
"My elders spoke Yiddish around the house when I was
little, so I understand it, some, and Yiddish isn't that far
from High Dutch."

Longarm allowed he'd heard as much.

Judy said, "After you'd been gone a time we served a late supper to the passengers of an eastbound night train, coming up out of the New Mexico Territory. Two men dressed like cowboys met an older man dressed more the way you are, right now, as he got off to stay in Trinidad. The three of them ordered coffee and donuts at the counter before they went on to wherever."

"Where does the Yiddish come in, Miss Judy?" he asked.

She said, "They weren't speaking Yiddish. They were speaking High Dutch. I don't think one of them understood it any better than me. But I think the one who'd already been in Trinidad a while didn't want to be overheard as he reported to what seemed to be a leader."

Longarm nodded and said, "In High Dutch. How much of it were you able to follow, Miss Judy?"

She said, "Well, *langarm* was duck soup easy, seeing I'd just met and talked to you again tonight. After that I was able to figure out that *dreifach* meant three times while *milchzug* could only mean milk train!"

Beth Ferguson said, "As soon as she got home to the dorm to tell me what she'd overheard I knew it couldn't wait until morning, improper as this all may seem!"

Longarm said, "You done right, Miss Beth. Go on, Miss Judy."

The younger Harvey gal said, "I wasn't able to follow word by word as I pretended not to be paying attention. Some of the words are not at all alike. But if I understood at all right the new arrival was worried about you more than he was one last ride. He said it this way. *Unser letzreiten.* Our last ride, if you want to get literal."

Longarm said, "I'd rather know what in blue blazes they were *planning* for that last ride, seeing they're so worried about my knowing!"

She said, "One of the riders who met the train said not to worry about you. I wasn't able to find out why. Oh, they *did* make mention of a milk train stop at a place they called *Das Kreuzschleppeschlucht*."

Longarm shook his head to say, "If there's one thing I know for certain about that milk train, I know it stops at no such place. I've been making notes."

Beth Feguson suggested Judy translate the outlandish notion into something more like English.

Judy thought and decided, " 'Cross dragging gulch' works. Sort of."

Longarm nodded firmly and said, "I know the place. It's Mexican name would be *El Barranco de Crucifixiónes*. It's a Penitente flag stop. It ain't been hit yet. Did they say they meant to hold a milk train there this coming weekend, Miss Judy?"

She said, "No. That's why we thought it too important to wait. The one who came in from further down the line agreed you in particular were starting to crowd them with talk of fast horses riding the Saturday morning train. So they mean to hit it this side of Friday at that place you schleppe the crosses!"

Longarm nodded, thought, and said, "It's Wednesday morning as we speak! So it's been nice talking to you, ladies, but this child has some *riding* in mind for what's left of the time I may have to work with!"

He tore upstairs to change back into riding duds, make sure his sixgun and Winchester were fully loaded, and toted his saddle and bridle through the early morning darkness to that same livery.

The owner was home in bed, of course. But the young Mex on duty knew who Longarm was and rustled him up as good an Arab-Morgan cross as they'd ever had when Longarm said he was serious.

The chunky but spunky black stud with four white stockings answered to the name of Diablito and the Mex advised a Spanish spade bit. Longarm said he felt more in control with his own cavalry bit and bridle. The Mex said, "Not with this *caballo*, but suit yourself *El Brazo Largo!*"

So as soon as they had Diablito ready to ride, Longarm rode, first to the tracks over to the west and then down the service road following them south. The mountain air was crisp and Diablito was feeling frisky enough to test a strange rider.

As he coyly tucked his head under to see how Longarm's right boot tip tasted Longarm kicked him hard in the muzzle, which inspired him to buck, as if he meant it.

Longarm stayed on, of course, as the aptly named Little Devil sun-fished and crow-hopped off-road through low chaparral, as if to deposit Longarm not-so-gently in the trackside tangle of varied but universally thornsome vegetation. But after a time, as Longarm just stayed put, heavier than a heap of riders he'd thrown in the past, Diablito decided he'd gripped the curb bit in his clenched teeth long enough and tried to settle back to a grudging trot.

Longarm wouldn't let him. Whipping his Stetson back and forth across the pony's ears as he hammed its ribs with his boot heels, Longarm let fly, "Powder River and let her buck! You spoiled rotten waste of fodder and water! You want to buck, let's *buck*! Was that the best you could do, you fat-ass stable pussy?"

It wasn't. Diablito had some more spite left in him. So the next mile or more south was rough on both of them as Diablito tried alternate good behavior with sneaky bucking until, seeing "horse sense" meant exactly what it sounded like, they began to get along better.

But by then Longarm was sore at himself for ignoring that good advice about spade bits back at the livery. Diablito wasn't a thoroughbred to begin with, even if he'd been trustworthy. But when a man has to ride on short notice he rides what he can get and he had a hell of a ways to go if he meant to get to *El Barranco de Cruci-*

fixiónes ahead of that morning milk train. He knew that even as he rode south from Trinidad the train he hoped to intercept would be starting its run down in New Mexico Territory. Stopping all along the way but moving way faster between time to reach that Penitente flag stop when, around five-thirty? That sounded about right and, shit, it was going on five already!

There was nothing he could do about that but ride on, and on some more, as the moon went down behind the mountains to the west whilst the starry sky commenced to get oyster gray above the ink-black eastern horizon.

Then Longarm spotted what seemed a star too bright and too close to the ground down the tracks ahead and whipped Diablito into full gallop with the rein ends, grunting, "That's her, stopped where I was hoping to get to first!"

As he rode in at full gallop with his Winchester '73 held like a big pistol in his free hand, he saw figures on the service road ahead. He called out, "I'd be the law! Just got a tip you might be held up here!"

A disgusted voice called back, "A lot you know! The cocksuckers already stopped us. Then one of them said he was sorry he'd got the dates mixed up and promised to settle with us Friday morning, somewheres else!"

Another railroader waved something in his hand, it wasn't light enough yet to make things out, and said, "They rode through them Mex jacals out of sight to the west, the crazy bastards! Scared the shit out of us and made us late again for no blamed reason at all! What in the fuck could they be *after*?"

Longarm said he'd ask them as he swung his mount that way. As he lit out to the west somebody called after him, "There are four of them! All four waving pisolivers, Lawman!"

Longarm didn't answer. He'd already known that and . . . Judy Gross had said a *fifth* one had arrived earlier that night. So where was at least one of a gang of at least five?

"Mastermind. We're getting to the endgame," Longarm decided as he tore through the little trackside hamlet at a lope. He called out to an old Mex in an open doorway and the Mex yelled back, *"¡Ellos irse por alli!"* So Longarm rode on, trusting the eyes of a pony that didn't much like him as they tore along a strange dark wagon trace.

He knew they'd have him outlined against the dawn if they reined in and they'd already proven a certain sincerity of intent with two nail bombs. But a lawman who didn't chase outlaws just because they might kill him didn't figure to catch many and, as he rode further up what now shaped up to be indeed a barranca or gulch, he kept spotting more and more detail, albeit nothing more interesting than the wagon ruts ahead weaving through goat-broused weeds closer in and low-chaparral farther up the slopes to either side. You didn't see trees of any size this close to a flag stop.

By the time it was almost light enough to see colors Longarm spotted movement ahead and rode off to one side to sit Diablito with his saddle gun loaded and locked across his knees until he saw it was a hay wagon drawn by a team of six and driven by a gal in once-newer flamenco skirts and a black rebozo framing her dark face. Longarm ticked his hat brim and asked if she'd seen any other Anglo riders that morning.

He naturally asked in Spanish to be told in the same lingo how four *Gringos chingado* had not only spooked her team and nearly spilled her load but accused her of being old and ugly.

Longarm agreed, since he couldn't clearly see all that much of the bare legs she'd hoisted her shabby skirts to reveal, that they'd likely been just guessing. He rode on as she asked him why he was in such a hurry and, for all he knew, she might have been pretty.

Birds were twittering and those big gray grasshopers with black and yellow butterfly wings were spooking Diablito from time to time by exploding from the dusty ruts ahead with their rattlesnake buzzing, the useless sons of bitches.

The walls of the barranca kept getting steeper and closer, shaping up more as a canyon as he probed its depths. He could see colors now and the stars had winked off in the ever lighter sky above. As the first rays of sunlight painted long shadows of himself and his mount in the dust ahead, Longarm spotted what could have been taken for a Mexican religious notion in painted plaster up the slope to his left. But at second look he saw it wasn't painted plaster. It was real flesh and blood. They'd nailed the poor bastard to a cross facing north because he'd have died in a day facing south this late in the spring.

Longarm reined Diablito off the wagon trace at an angle to approach the Penitente at a walk, braced for his mount to spook, as horseflesh tended to at the smell of blood.

The scrawny, nearly naked Mexican mestizo or full-blood was about forty with streaks of gray in his bushy hair and full beard. He'd shit himself down one leg past the hem of his burlap loin cloth. He wasn't nailed up the way you saw depictions of Jesus on the cross in painted plaster. A Jesuit physician Longarm knew who'd studied more than most on the topic had explained the way the Romans had really done it, the cruel-hearted bastards.

That form of public execution had never been meant to look dignified. It had been meant to hurt. A lot. So like the figures you saw in Papist churches, the volunteer ahead was cheating a mite with his feet nailed to that sort of step with two separate spikes.

The ropes binding his upper arms to the cross bar, close to his armpits, helped him stay alive as well. The way the real and way meaner Romans had done it hadn't made as pretty a picture.

They'd started with the man, woman, or child to be executed, bless their notions of blind justice, flat on their backs to be nailed to the cross bar through their wrists, not their palms, with wooden washers to keep the nails from pulling out. Then they'd bent the victim's knees up and forced their thighs apart, less dignified than you saw in church, so's they could drive one spike through both crossed heel bones before they stood the cross erect and gave the victim the swell choices of hanging by the wrists, unable to breathe, or pushing down with painfully pierced heels to breathe in agony. Longarm's Jesuit pal thought the Roman soldier who'd lanced Jesus in the side had been trying to do Him a favor. Crucified men had usually lasted longer on their crosses.

Reining in near the Penitente, Longarm called out, "*Buendias, Señor*. Have you been there long?"

The crucified Mexican croaked, "I have another day for to go. You seek, Señor, four Anglo riders who passed this way just as the moon was setting?"

Longarm said, "I am. I am the law and they just stopped a train down to the east. Could you use some canteen water, *amigo mio*?"

The Mexican shook his head and said, "No thank you, my brother. I have not suffered enough yet. I saw the riders you are after, as I said, by moonset. Was getting too dark for to make things out down there on *el camino* when I heard a wagon pass by, later."

Longarm nodded and said, "A hay wagon, driven by one of your kind. She said they'd passed her on the road, farther west, as it works out with your seeing them by moonlight and missing her. How much farther west does that wagon trace run?"

The Mexican said, "I am not certain. I have never been crucified up this barranca before."

A far less gentle voice called out, "Hey, gringo, for why you bother a holy man who seeks salvation? You wish for to die and go to hell with the rest of your kind, *pendejo chingado*?"

Longarm turned in the saddle to stare back the way he'd just come at the Mexicans on foot, a heap of Mexicans on foot, heading his way through the low chaparral with machetes, other agricultural tools, and more than one shotgun.

Not a one of them looked at all happy to see him that morning.

Chapter 11

Some of them still didn't feel it was right, but a suffering saint got to have the Indian sign on cultist with more natural feelings. So after their crucified holy man said Longarm was *"simpatico,"* and only out to arrest his own kind they grudgingly told him to just get the hell out of there. So he said, "Before I ride on, how far does that wagon trace run and what am I likely to run into up ahead?"

A kid who identified himself as a goatherd told him there was about three quarters of a gringo mile to go before it ended in a natural bowl as a dead end. The kid said, "An *hombre* on foot can climb out, but not with his caballo. You think they will leave four caballos there for you, Gringo?"

Longarm said there was only one way to find out and rode on before they could change their minds.

Knowing other lawmen would be possed-up by now lent an urgency to his otherwise cautious advance. Unless he could pin those mystery riders down he didn't want any other Anglo riders tangling with those Penitentes.

So he loped half a mile, reined in off the wagon trace, and tethered Diablito to some rabbit bush to crab even farther up to his left and work his way along the slope with his Winchester '73 at port with a round in the chamber.

The rising sun illuminated the far slope more, but he still felt as exposed as he wanted to be, moving smoothly instead of in eye-catching leaps and bounds. He dropped behind a swell outcrop of bedrock to catch his breath and get his bearings before he removed his hat and risked a peek.

The goatherd had told the simple truth. Longarm could see at a glance how the already wispy wagon ruts petered out in five or six acres gone to grass and such in a sort of natural bull ring formed by steep and then steeper rocky bluffs. There was no cover ahead for anyone to hide out behind. Longarm still held his saddle gun at port as he jogged down into the bowl to scout for signs. He was in a hurry but he had hardly any trouble finding nothing much.

There were horse apples, fresh and stale, scattered around. The grass, still green, had been worked over in pie slices by a scythe, with some cut hay still spread to dry on its own stubble. He decided the hay that Mex gal had been hauling had been cut and dried earlier. She likely meant to come back to rake the still curing hay and cut some more. She'd been helping herself to wild fodder on unclaimed land. She'd been lucky in loading up and hauling out before those rude mystery riders had shown up. Outlaws finding even a homely gal alone and helpless out in the middle of nowhere could get even ruder. But where in blue thunder *were* the sons of bitches?

Scouting the bases of the bluffs where the grass grew thicker offered no sensible suggestions. There was no way to scramble a shod horse up such slopes without leaving a sign. So what was left, a secret trap door out in the middle? Close at hand, the damned grass was cropped just above its roots and none of the grass grew tall enough to hide anything bigger than a rabbit holding its breath.

Shaking his puzzled head, Longarm jogged back to

Diablito, untethered the spunky stud, and forked himself aboard to lope back down the gulch with his Winchester out of its boot.

He heaved a sigh of relief as he passed the crucified Penitente with a wave of the Winchester. The stoic volunteer seemed alone up yonder in spite of the chaparral on the slope around him being less than stirrup high. Longarm had read how whole clans of Scotch highlanders could hug the ground in knee-deep heather to surprise the English. Longarm was out to prevent religious fanatics and a wound-up posse from surprising the shit out of one another.

Longarm was *simpatico* or open-minded to the Lakota Sundance, the Hopi Snakedance, and other such notions as long as nobody expected him to join in. He didn't try to understand them. Like he'd told that Chinese gal who considered his habit of eating butter purely disgusting, it was all in the way folk were brought up and had he said a word about her folk dining on dog meat?

Like a lot of Mex notions, the Penitente cult was more Indian than Spanish. The Archbishop of Mexico had asked them to cut it out and the Vatican had condemned the practice as downright presumptuous as well as crazy. But Los Penitentes assured everybody they never presumed to be crucified on Good Friday and usually chose the Saint's Day of the old boy they were nailing up.

Once he'd shared the suffering of his Lord as long as he could stand it, usually less than the three days maximum his fellows allowed before he had to come down from the cross ready or not, the surviving holy man, like a Lakota bearing the chest scars of the Sundance skewers, had more prestige than mere mortals and in the case of Los Penitentes, was often inclined to good works, such as food baskets for the poor, slathering a fresh coat of 'dobe where it was needed or beating the shit out of a wife beater. The decent things they did made up for the crazy ways they often acted to folk along both slopes of the Sangre de Cristos.

Mexican Indian folk, least ways.

Nailing folk to crosses, even when they asked you to, was against statute law in both Colorado and New Mexico Territory. The Sundance and Snakedance were forbidden as well. Though white Pentacostal Fundamentalists were allowed to let little kids pick up live diamondbacks, further east.

So when Longarm met up with the posse from Trinidad, not far from where he'd met that gal driving the hay wagon before dawn, he reined in on the wagon trace ahead of them and waved them down with the muzzle of his saddle gun, yelling, "They got away again. Don't ask me how. I still say it's impossible, even though three seperate witnesses told me I was right on their tails!"

The senior county lawman in command wanted to press on and scout for signs. Longarm said, "Already have. Let's talk private."

As the two of them drew off to one side Longarm quietly explained why they didn't want a mixed gaggle of lawmen, townsmen, and cowboys tearing up the wagon trace within sight of that crucified Penitente.

As Longarm had hoped, the undersheriff, a few years older than himself, had gotten to be an undersheriff by spending some time in Las Animas County without fucking up.

He muttered, "I hate it when them greasers carry on like that. It ain't natural. My old woman is Eye-talian Catholic, same as her Pope, and she says she never heard of lay folk or even clerics carrying on like that, and Eye-talians tell the same joke about wondering how Jesus could have been Jewish with such a Mexican name. You're sure there wasn't no sign up ahead?"

Longarm said, "If there was I missed it. I'm human. But I've done some scouting and when you don't see nothing but horse apples in five or six acres of wild hay,

93

much of it mowed, it's a safe bet there ain't no horses there. I just said I don't know how they got them up the steep bluffs all around. Only way out was back down the wagon trace leading in to the sort of natural soup bowl. Neither I nor two seperate witnesses I met along the way *saw* them headed back down the wagon trace. What say we tell everybody we want to make sure the milk finally got to town this morning?"

The undersheriff said, "Seems like more fun than a tangle with Mexican lunatics. But I hope you understand I'm sure you missed something?"

Longarm slid his Winchester back in its boot behind the right cheek of his rump as he replied, "Of course I missed something. I was there. This vaudeville gal who worked in a magic act once told me how stage magicians just hate to work orphan asylums and private birthday parties for rich kids because children don't pay proper attention and it's way tougher to *misdirect* 'em. Misdirection is when the magician gets everybody to look one way whilst he does something else in another direction. This gal complained how just as the magician is asking everybody to look in his hat and make sure it's empty some kid in the audience is likely to ask his momma why that lady is holding a white rabbit behind her back by the ears and so on."

The undersheriff called out, "We're headed back to the tracks, boys. Powell, you take the lead!"

As he and Longarm brought up the rear the older lawman asked, "Is that what you think they done, just now? Got us to look in an empty hat whilst they . . . what?"

Longarm said, "Don't know. I ain't young or innocent. I was looking where they wanted me to look."

"But you said there were other witnesses," the local lawman protested.

Longarm nodded and said, "All responsible adults, gazing after what they said they took for four riders in tricky light. Remember, *I* never saw *one* of them. An old

Mex near the tracks aimed them up this gulch for me. A Mex gal I met the way he said they'd gone told me they'd passed her in poor light and kept going. A mighty uncomfortable Penitente told me he'd made their outlines out just about moonset. Couldn't say the color of one mount. You ever see one of them oriental shadow shows like they put on at state fairs along with hoochy kootchy dancing and bagpipe music? You watch from the dark side of this lamp-lit screen and they throw all these shadows of puppet folk, lions, tigers, dragons, and such against the screen from the far side with paper cut-outs moving around on sticks."

The undersheriff scoffed, "Aw, come on, are you trying to sell me four paper puppets on sticks stopping another milk train and galloping up this way in the moonlight?"

Longarm said, "Of course not. I'm saying they'd been making others see things the way they *ain't*. There has to be a *point* to all this pointing us the wrong way. An informant I talked to earlier may or may not have spotted a mastermind or puppet master coming up out of New Mexico on a more serious train and, being of the Hebrew persuasion and able to follow the drift of a conversation they thought was private . . ."

"You suspect this whole thing's some Jewish plot?" the older lawman cut in.

Longarm said, "They were talking in High Dutch. One or more could be immigrants. Or they could be Pennsylvania Dutch from before the Revolution. I mean to ask 'em when we catch 'em. The point is that from the description she gave we're dealing with grown men, not wild kids, who've got something more serious than the morning milk in mind!"

The undersheriff asked who his she-male informant might be. Longarm knew he'd know Alda Grey had left town and that nobody in Trinidad knew all that much about a Denver insurance gal. So he misdirected the older lawman by saying, "Don't know where she might be right now. She said she overheard them plotting in High Dutch around the railroad depot."

And that had been the pure truth when you studied on it.

The ride back to Trinidad along the service road on jaded mounts took 'til close to ten. It was after ten by the time Longarm had congratulated that old Mex on Diablito and toted his saddle on back to his hotel.

There were no messages at the desk for him. He waved the bell hop off and lugged the heavily laden McClellan up the stairs to the third floor himself. By the time he reached the top landing he was cussing his fool self for not having the sense to get through life the easy way.

He shifted the saddle to his other hip as he moved along the hallway. He could see the waxed white stem of the match he'd left lodged in his door hinge long before he got there.

He lowered the saddle silently to the hall runner a good five paces short and quietly drew his six-gun as he moved in on the balls of his booted feet.

The intruder could have picked the lock and then re-locked it from the far side or, more likely just picked it. It was tougher to lock up than unlock with your average skeleton key or knitting needle.

Covering the door with the revolver in his right hand, Longarm put his tingling left hand to the cold brass knob and when nothing happened he began to gingerly twist the same. The well-oiled latch moved silently, Lord love it, as it proved to be unlocked. Later, of course, they'd work out how his uninvited visitor had seen the knob turning from the far side.

All Longarm knew, when first he flung the door open and chased his gun muzzle inside, fast and low, was that someone was just inside the door, outlined darkly by the brighter window light from behind. So the two of them went reeling across the rug to crash down together across the bed as Longarm hung on with one hand, raised the heavy six-gun high with the other, and yelled, "You move one fucking muscle and I'll bash your cocksucking skull in, junior!"

Then he saw he hadn't pinned a way smaller man to the mattress at all and said, "Oops, I'm sorry, Miss Ruth, I thought you were somebody else!"

The dishwater blond Widow Fenton gasped, "I never would have guessed! Was that any way to . . . Never mind. It was my fault. I *guess* it was my fault. I asked the maid who let me in to leave word for you at the desk and I assume she never?"

Longarm set the six-gun aside on the rumpled covers as he told her he suspected the maid couldn't have. He added, "No harm done and there's hardly call for you to be *crying*, Miss Ruth. I said I was sorry for calling you a . . . never mind."

She sobbed, "I'm not crying because you called me a cocksucker. I'm crying because some cocksucker is trying to put me out of business! Not content with stalling my morning milk, somebody just left a dead rat in a milk can and I feel so helpless and . . . Would you either get that fresh hand out from under my skirts or *move* it right, Custis?"

He smiled down sheepishly to say, "Sorry. It just seemed the natural place to put a free hand, once we found ourselves in this unexpected position."

She sighed and said, "I know. I was happily married for some time and that *does* feel so . . . natural. But don't you think we ought to shut the door, now, Custis?"

He sighed and rolled off, parting being such sweet sorrow once you'd had your hand on first base, and said, "I got a saddle and bridle out in the hall to worry about, too. Don't go 'way. I'll be right back."

He naturally expected her to have cooled off and crossed her legs by the time he could drop the saddle and bridle just inside and then shut and bar the door. But as

Ruth Fenton would be telling him later as they shared a smoke, it had been a spell since she'd been happily married and she didn't want to do another thing but fuck like a mink until going on high noon.

Chapter 12

Like many gals who'd kept their teen-aged figures well into their thirties, Ruth Fenton was built more firmly than a lot of her milk-fed customers and, as Longarm had certainly enjoyed learning for himself, nine out of ten widow women who'd been happily married up with a man they'd admired gave a hell of a better ride than many a divorcee who'd never been able to get along with the shiftless skunk who'd broken her in and taught her the little she knew about the subject.

They were going at it dog-style, the best position for combining conversation with sexual congress, by the time Ruth told him why she'd been so sure somebody was trying to put her out of business. She said she'd had her help dump the whole shipment from that one farm after pouring a dead rat head first from a delivery can into one of her glass bottles.

Gripping her firmly but gently by her trim hip bones as he stood with his bare feet planted widely on the rug beside his bed, Longarm said, "Rats do manage to drown themselves, scampering around a dairy barn in the dark, and the way I understand it, none of those mystery riders have ever boarded a milk car with or without a dead rat handy."

She arched her slender waist to reply, "Ooooh, more to the right and are you saying it's impossible I'm the one they're after, then?"

Shifting his approach to the angle she indicated Longarm told her, "So far the big loser has been the railroad. You've made a modest *profit* on milk deliveries you whittled the price down on. The farmers you paid less passed their losses on to the AT&SFRR local division and they in turn passed *their* losses on to their insurance underwriters."

He let that sink in for a couple more thrusts and added, "After that we ain't talking about the national debt. Regular train robbers would have taken more off just the *passengers* of a serious cross-country train than those bozos have ridden off with after stopping the morning milk train four times. The figures are easy to add up because so far they've yet to demand the brakeman's swell railroad watch! Let's turn over so's I can kiss you some more, now."

They did and lost track of the thread of the conversation for a time as she caught up on what she said she hadn't been indulging in for quite some time.

Gals always said that. But it seemed logical a woman running her own business in a man's world would have to be careful, next to a lawman with a tumbleweed job, who she got in bed with. He knew a mighty lusty Texas gal with over a hundred healthy young hands on her payroll and she swore she'd never even danced with one of 'em.

You could ask a man to bust a bronc or steam clean a dairy or you could ask a man to get on top and do you right. You had a time finding a man as willing to put his heart and soul into both chores for the same gal.

After they'd come that way and wound up cuddled up at the head of his bed, she said she didn't smoke but didn't mind if he did, she remembered what she'd come for, before they'd started coming, and asked what Longarm thought those outlaws wanted, if putting her out of business wouldn't work.

He finished lighting his cheroot, shook out the match, and cuddled her closer as he confessed, "I haven't been able to come up with a sensible motive. I'd be certain they were just fool kids out for a game of cops and robbers but for two things. Whether those are cap pistols they've been waving or not, those dynamite bombs were meant serious."

She draped a naked knee over Longarm's thigh as she asked what the second clue might be.

Reminding himself to watch his stray thoughts around a sharp business woman, Longarm said, "Never mind the details and suffice it say a grown man in a grown-up-three-piece suit, reading like a gunslick because he won't work as a lawman, met a couple of younger but full-grown riders answering to the general description of all four train robbers, to not only mention me by name but allow they were about set for their final ride."

Ruth asked, "Wasn't that last night, then?"

He said, "At face value, yep. At *sensible*, nope. Last night reads as a diversion. Knowing everyone was expecting them to stop the milk train a fourth time this coming weekend, they stopped it last night instead, as if taunting us, to take nothing of value from anybody, ride nowheres in particular, and vanish into thin air some more. It's as if they've been trying to establish some sort of *tradition*, as profitless but certain as those local Penitentes you see from a train window now and again in these parts."

She slithered her naked thigh along his, to their mutual enjoyment, as she asked, "Do you think it's possible those predawn mystery riders are tied in some way with mysterious Mexicans? I've heard something about the one of them letting fly a *gallo del ranchero* taunt as they ride off."

He replied, "At least two of them speak High Dutch

101

and once you've heard that Mex version of the rebel yell you don't need to speak Spanish to fake one. Los Penitentes can act mighty strange or even ornery now and and again, but the cult ain't into banditry. They're into the Ten Commandments past common sense and why would one nailed-up Penitente and two likely Mex admirers have told me which way the outlaws I was chasing rode?"

She answered, simply, "What if all three of them lied?"

He started to object, stared thoughtfully, and took the smoke from his teeth to kiss her warmly before he said, "I just found out what that Englishman who tried to patent his own lightbulb a week after Mister Edison must have felt like! It's no wonder you own the biggest dairy in Trinidad, you smart little gal!"

She smiled up at him uncertainly to ask what she'd said so smart.

He said, "Misdirection and the rules of evidence. This magical gal I used to know explained how most stage magic never needs all the trap doors and invisible wires folk imagine and the rules of evidence, or the process of eliminating, calls for setting aside the more complicated anwer in favor of the more simple one."

She snuggled closer and confided she had no idea what he was talking about. He said, "Let's start with complicated. Me chasing four riders I can't see up a dead-end wagon trace, encouraged to do so by three Mex witnesses I've never met before, until I arrive at break of day at the end of their trail and they just ain't there. That sound complicated enough for you?"

She said it sounded impossible.

He said, "I know. Try her your simple way. I come loping along in the pre-dawn dark to be told by likely trustworthy railroad men four rascals have done it again and galloped west. So far so good because if *everybody's* lying and no mystery riders have ever stopped the morning milk trains we're in real trouble!"

She said she knew some of the crew aboard the morning milk trains.

He said, "Bueno. I never laid eyes on that old Mex by the flag stop, waving me up that wagon trace. So he could have been fibbing. Or he could have been telling it the way he'd seen it. They could have turned off the wagon trace long before the gully walls to either side got steep enough to matter. Then I met a Mex gal driving a hay wagon down from gathering wild hay and had no reason to suspect she lied when she said the four of 'em were still out ahead of me. That leaves the Penitente I took for a mighty sincere Christian. I hate to think he told me a bare faced lie. But if he saw four riders headed up a blind alley and never saw them coming out he saw something impossible, Dad blast Thomas Jefferson!"

The thigh-slithering blonde asked how Thomas Jefferson figured in any pre-dawn pursuits of mystery riders.

Longarm blew smoke out both nostrils and explained, "He was smart as a whip and inclined to think scientifical when he had to weigh logical against illogical answers. So one day they came to him with reports by two Harvard professors who'd witnessed a meteor shower and gathered up rock-solid evidence that white-hot rocks had indeed come sizzling down from the sky, as astronomers had been arguing back and forth for years."

She said, "Everybody knows about meteorites, dear. Didn't they gather bushels of the things after that famous meteor shower of 1836? I remember hearing my elders talking about it. They said it looked like the sky was falling all across the land!"

He said, "I missed it because I hadn't been born yet. Thomas Jefferson missed it because he'd been dead ten years. He went to his grave convinced shooting stars were optical illusions because, he said, it was easier to believe two Harvard professors would lie than it was to believe rocks fell out of the sky."

She had to think about that before she decided, "You're

saying three lying witnesses make more sense than vanishing horses. But you mean to concede . . . what? Vanishing horses?"

He shrugged his bare shoulder under her soft cheek and said, "Makes no real sense either way, but liars ain't as impossible as four vanishing horses, at least until you consider the man who vanished around the horses!"

She rolled half atop him to reach down between them as she languidly asked what on earth he was talking about now.

Longarm said, "Let me finish this smoke. They taste awful when you relight 'em. The man who walked around the horses is a famous and true mystery, authenticated by the British Diplomatic Corps. Happened during a lull in the Napoleonic Wars. This English diplomatic courier was on his way somewhere by mail coach, riding with friends and friendly stangers as far as anyone knows, when they pulled into a regular stage stop to change teams whilst the passengers stretched their legs or had a bite inside. The passengers in the crowded coach got out both sides, of course. The Englishman got out on the side facing road traffic and walked around the horses as they were being unhitched. That's it."

She asked, "What was it?" as she began to stroke it.

He snuffed his cheroot to get a better grasp of the situation as he told her, "That was the last anyone ever saw of the man who walked around the horses to this very day. He never made it into the stage stop. He never got back in the coach. He was just gone. End of the story. Albeit the case is still open in the files of Scotland Yard."

As he proceeded to remount her, Ruth demanded, "Wait! Tell me the weanie! What really happened to the man who walked around the horses?"

As he rubbed the head of his new inspiration up and down betwixt her love lips he insisted, "Nobody knows. True story. We'll *never* know the answer at *this* late date, but it seems clear they must have missed the way things really happened. Had I been there I'd have wanted to know who *said* he walked around the horses. Everybody from his coach wouldn't have been watching. When he never joined the rest of them inside somebody would have asked where he was. Then somebody else lied deliberate or made a wild guess. As soon as you allow he might have headed off in *any* direction you can forget secret trap doors in a public highway and study one who might have marched him where for what reason."

As he entered her again they both forgot all about the never-to-be-solved mystery of the man who walked around the horse. He had enough more recent puzzles to solve and she was losing interest in the milk train mystery if that rat hadn't been drowned in her milk on purpose.

When they came back up for air again she asked if he still thought they'd stop the Friday night-Saturday morn milk train as they had before.

He said, "Don't know. Got to figure they might."

She said, "I'm trying to work out our own little secrets. I know you don't believe this, but I really came here this morning to talk to you about that rat in my morning milk!"

He kissed her reassuringly, leaving it in her to soak as he told her he'd already said he was sorry for jumping all over her. When he asked what else was so complicated Ruth explained, "Company at my house, ex–in–laws from back east. I don't think they'd understand what we've been up to at all!"

Longarm smiled thinly and said, "Most everybody *understands*. They don't always *approve* anybody but themselves getting away with it. Are you saying you don't want me calling on you with flowers, books, and candy, Miss Ruth?"

She shuddered, "Perish the thought! We're going to have to be very, very careful, Custis. I'd just die if word got out about us!"

He hesitated, decided anything he might say might hurt

105

her feelings as much and left it at Lady's Choice. She decided, "It might be best if we behaved ourselves until my in-laws went back east. It's awkward to run a business, show visitors around the Sangre de Cristos, and manage a secret love affair. But they'll be leaving in less than two weeks and we'll be free, free, free to see what . . . we shall see?"

Longarm kissed her some more. That seemed safer than anything she wanted him to say. She never said she was smart enough to know some things were best left unsaid. He got dressed and went out for some groceries whilst she snuck a bath none of her in-laws had to know about.

The plan was to picnic in bed and if they were wondering where she was, at her dairy, she could tell them most anything when and if she went back to work that afternoon.

But things didn't work out that way.

He'd loaded up on potato salad, cold cuts, and bottled beer and so he was looking forward to rejoining Ruth in his room. But as he was passing the desk they told him there was a message for him.

It was in a plain white envelope with neither a business letterhead nor return address. It was addressed to him in what looked like a man's handwriting. But you never knew and so, before taking it on up to open in front of possibly another woman, Longarm set their picnic cold cuts on the hotel desk to open and read the mysterious message.

It was from the railroad. Asking for a secret meeting at the depot. They said they were pretty sure they knew who'd been stopping those milk trains and why they'd been stopping them.

Chapter 13

It seemed only right to serve Ruth Fenton the late morning snack he'd promised her. After that it seemed only natural to get undressed for his just dessert. They still parted friendly but proper on the street out front as somewhere a church bell chimed twelve times. He had to offer but she refused his offer to walk her back to her dairy, even though it was partly along his way. It was the quiet man-eaters who acted the most proper in public, Lord love 'em.

The section security supervisor had signed his note Gilchrist, Warren H. Gilchrist, and from the way the note read Longarm figured he had to be that same railroad dick who'd only been funning when he'd promised those insurance folk he meant to eat cucumbers and do other wonders with a team of extra gun hands. He hadn't sounded all that worried about those milk train robberies, if that was what you called late milk deliveries. Longarm was anxious to hear what had inspired Gilchrist to take more interest all of a sudden.

But when he got there a homely gal who could have passed for old Henry at the home office wearing a gingham dress with his hair pinned up in a bun with a pencil stuck through it like a cannibal bone told Longarm her boss hadn't come back from his noon dinner yet.

Rather than spend an indefinite time staring at any gal that dolorous to stare at, Longarm allowed he'd be back and ducked out to explore the Union Station of Trinidad.

There wasn't much to explore. It was way smaller than the Union Station up Denver way. What he took at first glance for a cigar store Indian was seated cross-legged with his back against the bricks and a Navajo saddle blanket covered with Heap Big Injun shit spread on the slate walk in front of him.

In spite of the likely true claim they lost money on their passenger service, the Atcheson Topeka and the Santa Fe seemed out to promote the western tourist industry by encouraging everybody from Fred Harvey to a rapidly expanding Heap Big Injun tribe selling a mish-mash of arts, crafts, and local color. With results already deplored by serious students of the American Indian, as Zuni notions wound up on Navajo silversmithing, Pawnee beadwork on sort-of Lakota moccasins and all sorts of zigzags traditional Navajo weavers had never used on the now more flashy "Navajo blankets."

Longarm saw the simple saddle blanket of raw black, brown and white wool had to be a family heirloom, albeit a war trophy if he was right about the old man's leggings and breech clout, worn under an old cavalry shirt of faded blue, adding up to Tanoan, the nation you'd expect to find in the Sangre de Cristos. But some of the flashy baskets he had for sale, woven small for the tourist trade and not as tightly as any serious Indian basket, betrayed cottage industry if not mass production in their identical picky-picky thunderbirds, turtles, and such. The most outlandish items on sale were pasteboard display cards with stone arrowheads wired in place over printed captions describing them as Apache, Comanche, Kiowa, Sioux, and so forth.

Each display cost seventy-five cents. So Longarm bought one as an excuse to hunker down, strike up a conversation, and offer the old Tanoan a cheroot. They had to manage with baby-talk English. Longarm knew a few words and phrases in the Uto-Aztec of the Great Basin, the Sioux-Hokan of the Great Plains, and of course everybody knew some Algonquin because the early settlers on the eastern seaboard had met them first and thought *all* Indians wore *moccasins*, lived in *wigwams* with their *squaws*, and hit you up alongside the head with a *tomahawk* if you said you didn't care for more of the *succotash* the squaws had made for you, Pale Face.

Calling a Lakota *weya*, *winyan*, or worse yet a *wichincha* a *squaw* could get you hit up alongside the head indeed. White mountain men had brought the word "squaw" west to apply to the *wichincha* or flirty young gals sometimes treated rough by self-confident bullies with guns. The other terms just meant women, depending on how they were used.

Having no idea what you called a woman in Tanoan, Longarm didn't get into that with the old Railroad Station Indian. He was able to establish the older man as a trader from Taos who'd come this far east aboard the AT&SFRR. Longarm had no call to doubt the old Tanoan when he said he'd only recently arrived and had no idea where four riders could vanish into hogbacks and canyons he wasn't familiar with. He said none of his own kind had even hunted on the eastern slopes of the Sangre de Cristos since Spanish mission times. The Tanoans had played a leading part in the great uprising that had wiped out the first version of Santa Fe. Like most of the pueblo nations of the Upper Rio Grande the Tanoans had managed a tense armistice with the less dogmatic Spanish settlers who'd replaced earlier religious zealots and considered the Anglo-Americans who'd won that war with Mexico some improvement.

That was why Tanoans, Zuni, and such had wound up less famous than say Apache or Comanche. Having established in Old Spanish times that outsiders messed with pueblo customs at their own peril, they'd gotten along better than most Indians in the Southwest just by being easier for white folk to *understand*.

Unlike wandering hunter-gathering or raiding bands, the pueblo stayed put within posted boundaries an illiterate homesteader moving in just down the pike could savvy. No white man who wasn't looking for a fight wanted to ride through a hedged field planted to beans, corn, and squash and no pueblo youth was required to come home with a white man's horse or hair to be admired by the gals. Longarm's ears perked up when the old Tanoan opined *Los Penitentes* were way tougher to get along with. Longarm had heard from others how some of the more zealous Papists in the Sangre de Cristos were descended from tougher hold-outs who hadn't fled south to Old Mexico when the Pueblo Chief, Pope—and he'd meant that the way it sounded—had been nailing Spanish priests and nuns to trees, seeing they found that such a great honor.

Some Mexicans Longarm knew, albeit not Penitentes themselves, had told him the cult had been started by Spanish captives who'd lived through and escaped such Indian tortures to hide out, muster, and breed in the side canyons of the Sangre de Cristos. They hadn't explained how come most Penitentes seemed to be nigh-pure Mission Indian. Mexicans were less inclined than Anglos to notice faces off Aztec murals seated next to 'em in church.

Having satisfied himself it would likely be a waste of time to scout for a pueblo hide-out that far east, Longarm handed the old Indian a fresh cheroot and allowed he had to get back to work.

As he rose, the old Indian asked how come he'd bought that fool card of arrowheads, seeing he seemed to know more than most of his kind about real people. Longarm said he'd bought them for some white kids he knew and ambled on down to the Harvey House with the fool card.

Seated at a corner table he looked around for a waste

basket to toss his six-bits worth of nonsense into. He didn't see any. He began to pry the arrowheads off the card as he waited to be served. When a Harvey gal he hadn't talked to before came over to take his order and ask what he was doing, Longarm said, "I'd like a mug of black coffee and an unglazed donut whilst I kill some time here. Might as well hang on to these fool arrowheads for now. Don't ask me why. Prisoners killing time in jail or old Indians spitting and whittling out front of their trading post take as long as half an hour knapping one of these wicked looking things out of flint, chert and . . . this white one's agate. Ain't it pretty?"

The Harvey gal replied, "You're teasing, aren't you? I'd think you'd spend all day just chipping one of those points from solid *rock*!"

Longarm cheerfully replied, "*I* might take longer. I ain't an experienced flint knapper. Old-timers who still knap flints for heirloom rifles or Indians with nothing better to do can sort of whittle flint about as fast as a school-boy can whittle an elm-twig whistle. They hold the flint in slickery-proof leather with one hand and press tight with an elk-horn or bone point with the other. Can't use anything hard as steel lest the flint shatter. Like I said, it's a knack. As hard to explain as how some folk can brew coffee whilst others can't."

She said she could take a hint and dashed off to the kitchen whilst Longarm put his now-handier collection of half-ass arrowheads in a jacket pocket. He figured nobody would mind if he just left the empty card on the table to be cleaned off with the menu, used napkin, cup, and saucer.

He'd about forgotten he had the few ounces of rock on him by the time he'd killed half an hour nursing two cups of coffee and, what the hell, he always had room for a slice of marble cake.

When he tried at the security office some more that awful-looking gal showed him in to see that Warren

Gilchrist was indeed the same railroad dick he'd talked to earlier. The older man rose to shake and say, "Come along with me. Wait 'til I show you what we've got for you in the baggage room!"

As they entered the waiting room and crossed it to a side door leading behind the counter passengers checked baggage back and forth across, the railroad dick said, "I rode for the South, myself, but fair is fair and if I was running this railroad more than one man of the colored persuasion might be promoted higher."

They ducked into a larger than expected chamber out-fitted with floor to ceiling shelves, with about half of them jammed with baggage ranging from briefcases to steamer trunks, all tagged by AT&SFRR, D&RGRR or both. As a tall stooped-shouldered colored man with hair that looked like steel shavings turned from the checking counter to greet them, Gilchrist told Longarm, "It was Elisha, here, who spotted the peculiar pattern. Like I told you, before, I had it down as kid stuff until this morning."

Elisha Madison, as it turned out, didn't look as if he wanted to shake. He had the stiff correct manners of an old garrison trooper, or a former slave and, like the pueblo nation, tried to convey the silent message that he didn't want to marry your sister and vice versa. Leading the way to a compact but heavily built sea chest on a lower shelf, he explained, "You get passengers wanting things one way. You get passengers wanting things other ways. But there's ways that make sense and then there's ways that don't."

Longarm glanced down to see the sea chest had been checked in wearing a Denver & Rio Grande tag that had seen some travel. A spanking new Santa Fe tag was wired next to it on the same hand grip. Elisha said, "Came down from Denver, checked through to here. Owner came to the counter to say he needed some stuff out of it but wanted it stored here, AT&SF, 'til he was ready to board an eastbound with it, last night. When I asked was he a

112

traveling salesman he called me an uppity coon and told me it was none of my black beeswax and stormed out front with a bitty carpet bag."

Longarm said, "Some old boys are born stupid whilst others have to send away for lessons. What made you wonder if he might be a traveling salesman, Mister Madison?"

Elisha Madison said, "The way he was gadding across the map by rail. Who else would take a train south from Denver, stay over a short while and hop a train from here to Kansas City, northeast of these parts?"

Longarm said, "I follow your drift. He was already north of here when he hopped that southbound from Denver. Nobody going anywheres to *stay* a piece would follow such a peculiar route. Traveling salesman or a railroad-riding gambling man might wander about like that, though."

Gilchrist said, "It gets curiouser and curiouser, like Miss Alice said, when you wire Denver for his original string of tickets. Our Mister Toss, as he calls himself, paid the D&RGRR way more in Denver for a through ticket to El Paso. Like a man with a visit to Old Mexico in mind."

Longarm asked which train down from Denver they were talking about. When Gilchrist told him he nodded tersely and said, "He rode down aboard the same Monday afternoon train as me. When I got off here in Trinidad he did the same, making other plans as he rerouted this baggage. If he said he meant to come back for it last night he must have had another change of heart."

He reached for his pocket knife, saying, "I got a blade here a Denver locksmith said he wasn't supposed to grind for me."

The two railroad men exchanged glances. Gilchrist said, "Don't try to teach your granny how to suck eggs. Elisha, here, has to open unclaimed baggage all the time. So when the moody cuss who called him an uppity coon never came back for his baggage last night, the way he'd said he might . . ."

"What's in it?" Longarm cut in.

Elisha permitted himself a frosty smile as he unlocked the sea chest with a pass key of his own to fling the domed lid wide.

Longarm whistled as he stared down at the dynamite, a heap of dynamite along with caps and a coil of fuse, nestled amid clean shirts, socks, and a paperback edition of *Justine*, the dirtiest book ever written by the notorious Marquis de Sade.

Longarm mused, "He rerouted this sea chest to K.C. after he'd taken something out of it, eh? But he never came back like he said he aimed to?"

Gilchrist suggested, "He ain't done here in Trinidad and he took enough dynamite with him. Or he's afraid that having failed, twice, coming back here like a coyote-spooked jack rabbit circling its home range could be too big a boo when a man can always pick up more dynamite and even dirty books without half the risk."

Longarm wrinkled his nose to decide. "I reckon I might ask Detective Caruso if he has the manpower for a luke-warm stake-out."

Elisha asked, "Would it help if you knew where the travelsome Mister Toss asked a hack driver of my complexion to carry him after he'd told me to mind my own black beeswax?"

As the two white men stared flabbergasted, Elisha's faint smile reminded them of the Mona Lisa in blackface as he said, "When young Calvin Brown was next out front with his hack I took it upon my uppity self to ask where he'd taken the ofay mother, and I never called him mother *dear*. Calvin told me the kindly Mister Toss had carried his one carpetbag into the Posada de la Junta, run by Mexicans, near Linden and Main, out on the outskirts of town. Calvin said the ofay never tipped him for the ride. All this happened Monday morn, of course. So I can't say for certain our traveling Mister Toss would be there right now."

"Let's go find out!" said Warren Gilchrist with a wolfish grin.

To which Longarm could only reply, "Let's not chase rats through the stable with a shotgun. Don't want to spook the other rats he may be in the stable with. I'll mosey down that way by way of the first street to the south of Main, for openers."

Gilchrist swore and said, "It's time to posse up for a showdown! They know you on sight! You'll never round 'em all up yourself and can't you see why Toss brung all that dynamite down from Denver? All this bullshit with the milk trains has been for *practice*. Testing the waters on horseback for the job they've been planning all along!"

Chapter 14

Longarm said he was listening.

Gilchrist said, "They got everybody expecting a train robbery. A milk train robbery, say Saturday morn in the wee small hours. They got us sort of *trained* to chase 'em west into the box canyons of the Sangre de Cristo foot-hills. But Saturday, at the end of the month, is payday. Every bank in town will be cashing paychecks, making out money orders to send home and so forth. Are you with me so far?"

Longarm cautiously suggested he go on. Gilchrist said, "To have that much cash on hand on Saturday the banks will have called on the bigger banks in Denver, where they keep the federal mint making all that money, to feed the Trinidad kitty come *tomorrow*, being it's Thursday, because they need a couple of days to tally and distribute all them different payrolls."

"Where does Mister Toss and this dynamite come in?" asked Longarm.

Gilchrist said, "From Denver, the same as you. Toss was bringing all this boom-boom down here for his pals when he recognized you aboard that southbound D&RG day tripper and . . ."

"We're getting a mite complicated," Longarm cut in,

explaining, "I understand yet another member of whatever came up this way from parts *south* to join at least two riders answering to the descriptions given by their milk train victims. So now we got sinister strangers coming in from all over creation and I still don't see why they'd be in the market for all this dynamite!"

Gilchrist suggested, "To blow the safe the money from Denver will be riding south in! Ain't you never heard of blowing safes?"

Longarm nodded but said, "You do that with nitro-glycerine. Professional safe crackers or Yeggs mix their own or cook it, slow and gentle, out of dynamite sticks soaking in warm water. You only need a few sticks worth to squirt into the cracks of your average safe before you hit it with a nine-pound sledge. That leaves us all these extra sticks, after Mister Toss whipped up two separate dynamite bombs to toss my way. It works a tad better if we have the mysterious Mister Toss sincerely on his way to Old Mexico with a valuable asset to *La Revolución* that either side would pay a lot for. Then let's say he spotted this child, as you suggested, and got off in Trinidad with me, meaning to settle old scores."

"What scores might they be?" asked the railroad dick.

Longarm said, "I mean to ask him. Toss works better as the nickname for a bomb-throwing man than a family handle. He's proven he can't have much imagination. He's after me *personal*. I doubt it has anything to do with that payday money you mentioned. But it was a sharp mention. So why don't you check with your opposite number at the Denver & Rio Grande to make certain such a train may indeed be headed this way tormorrow!"

Gilchrist tried, "Hell, it stands to reason! All them banks have to get all that money from some damned where and the Denver mint is where the money grows!"

Longarm insisted, "Let's not stand on reason. Let's make *certain*. Banks do take it in and lay it out most every day of the month and we'd surely look silly getting all fired up about a money train that ain't coming!"

Gilchrist called Longarm a spoilsport but allowed he'd go have a jaw with the infernal Denver & Rio Grande. Longarm said they'd compare notes in the Harvey House around suppertime if they were both alive. Longarm felt no call to lay all his cards on the table just yet. It was his own beeswax how he worked and after that it was a pure pain trying to explain how he'd gotten to be *El Brazo Largo* to so many Mexicans north or south of the border.

Leaving the station on foot, Longarm naturally bee-lined to that same Mex livery, took the crusty old owner aside, and explained his need to pussyfoot around La Posada de la Junta.

As he'd hoped, all the Mexicans of substance around Trinidad being on speaking terms, the livery Mex knew the innkeeping widow who owned and operated what had once been a last-chance cantina for eastbound travelers on the Santa Fe Trail. Her name was Ramona Montoya and it was not true, as some said, she was half Apache. According to the livery owner she was merely a woman of some passion who demanded respect from her guests if they knew what was good for them.

When Longarm asked for suggestions as to how he ought to approach this woman of respect about an Anglo guest that might explode, the older man called into the darkness of his stable.

When a barefoot *mestizo* kid appeared with a manure fork in hand his boss gave him new chores he seemed to cotton to a whole lot better.

The Posada de la Junta was within the easy killing range for an army .45-70 if there hadn't been so much of El Corazon de Trinidad in the way and Longarm allowed he did better afoot in tight spots when he didn't have Black Beauty or any other pets to worry about. So the Mex kid, his nickname being Gordo, led Longarm east along the tree shaded Second Street as far as the north-west to southeast Linden Street. Two blocks short of

118

Main, Gordo left Longarm under the awning of a sidewalk *cantina* to pussyfoot on as Longarm smiled at his skinny ass. Longarm was smiling because "Gordo" translated roughly as "Fatso." Nicknames were like that. Sometimes they turned things upside down whilst other times they were on the money. "Toss" seemed a more telling description for a bomb-flinging son of a bitch. Longarm searched his memory in vain for outlaws of that handle as he nursed a *pulque* served by a glowing young gal with *Indio Puro* features. It was easy for an Anglo to nurse a *pulque*. It was a sort of beer brewed without distillation from the same agave as tequila. It took some getting used to. Some held it reminded them of flat beer with okra, or mayhaps warm spit, stirred in. Mexicans found it a tad stronger, or cheaper, than the *cerveza* that tasted much like any other beer.

Longarm still had some *pulque* left whilst he worked on a second cheroot by the time the skinny Gordo got back to tell him the coast was clear and the most respectable Ramona Montoya was most anxious for to meet a hero of *La Revolución*. As Longarm tagged along the kid explained there really was a Gringo guest answering to the name of Toss Turner booked into the posada up on Main. But he'd gone off somewhere and when they'd asked if he'd be back for supper he'd allowed he doubted it.

They still entered the rambling 'dobe posada by way of a gap in the cactus fence of the backyard. The most respectable Ramona Montoya was at her kitchen door, smiling fit to bust. Longarm found it easy to smile back. She seemed a woman of a certain age just pleasantly plump enough to smooth out any wrinkles that might have otherwise crept up on her. He could see she had enough Indian blood to show. But she was mostly that Spanish breed called Celtiberian, from up to the northwest corner of Old Spain where some said the Scotch Plaid and Tam O'Shanter hats had been invented back in pagan times before the Children of Dana had sailed off to occupy the Tin Islands in ships with painted leather sails. Some regular Irish looked sort of Spanish, too. So there was likely something to their old folk tales.

In sum, Ramona Montoya looked like you'd expect an Irish-Apache breed to come out, with smiling eyes as black as those polished volcanic glass pebbles the Heap Big Injun trade sold as "Apache Tears."

She invited them in, set them at a kitchen table painted electric blue and said she had her own help watching out front for Toss Turner from a second-story window next to his hired room.

When Longarm asked her if she'd let him search the suspect's room in his absence, feeling no call to discuss search warrants with an American citizen more comfortable speaking Spanish, she took him by one hand to drag him up the stairs after her, giggling like an Irish kid on Halloween.

The mysterious Toss Turner had only left that small carpetbag Elisha had mentioned near the foot of the bed. Longarm opened it. There wasn't anything more incriminating than some dirty shirts, clean socks and two more dirty books. Longarm told Ramona Montoya, "If he has any dynamite left he's packing it with him."

She asked Longarm if he'd blow the son of a bitch up out front instead of on her premises and added, "He is going for to blow up when you shoot him, no?"

Longarm said, "I hope I can take him alive. It's hard to make a man talk after you've blown him up."

He saw she still looked worried and soothed, "Dynamite ain't that easy to set off, Miss Ramona. The bombs I told you about downstairs were set off by lit fuses crimped to black powder caps stuck in the sort of putty mix of clay and nitroglycerine Mister Nobel invented. He invented it to make touchy nitro safer to handle. Takes a real jar, like a black powder cap going off like a shotgun shell to detonate dynamite, see?"

She asked, "What if you shoot it with a bullet?"

He said, "I'll try not to. Like I said, I want a word with the cuss about his surly manners. I've never heard of any outlaw called Toss Turner. So it's still up for grabs why he's been so surly on two separate occasions here in Trinidad."

She suggested they lay for the cuss in the *sala* next door in case he got past her scattered look-outs. Longarm put the carpetbag back the way he'd found it and followed her into the unlet quarters right next door. As they entered she told the pretty little thing peering through the window curtains to go down to the stairwell and give a holler if that gringo chingado got past the kids downstairs.

Longarm took her place behind the thin muslin curtains. He saw that, thanks to the old posada having been there before they'd unkinked and gravel-paved that stretch of a wagon trace into a straighter city street, the posada sat at just the right angle to offer him a swell field of fire into the Corazon de Trinidad, with clear shots at the walks to either side of Main Street as things calmed down after dinnertime for a sort of compromise siesta.

Folk who'd never dwelt in the dry sunny climes Spanish-speaking folk seemed to fancy tended to fancy *la siesta* as a lazy no-good greaser custom. But any Anglo with a lick of sense who lived through more than one serious southwestern summer learned to go along with his Mex neighbors a mite. It was too much to expect late Victorians raised on the Protestant work ethic to shut a town down *total* from noon to say three-thirty or four, but by half-past-one wagon traffic had died off down yonder and only a very few stubborn souls with urgent errands were to be seen, now, walking on the shady south side of the street.

The pleasantly plump Ramona shut and barred the door as she went on about it being such an honor for to fight *ladrones* with *El Brazo Largo* and moved closer to sit at the foot of the neatly made bed for hire as she asked if it was true he'd been the lover of the notorious *La Mariposa* south of the border that time.

When he modestly replied no true *caballero* ever spoke about a *mujer* when she wasn't there to defend herself, Ramona sighed and said, "They say the two of you made furious love and died together over and over in that railroad signal tower as you were waiting for to derail that troop train for *La Causa*! Is true?"

Longarm laughed despite himself and replied, "Gossip about this child seems to be as wild north or south of the border. Like I keep trying to tell *Los Rurales* down Mexico way, I never set out to overthrow anybody's Stable Government, as Washington keeps describing it in spite of its bad smell. I've just found it sort of hard to get along with Mexico's answer to our Texas Rangers. I never shot a *rurale* who wasn't out to shoot me as I was trying my best to get along down yonder."

She said, "They say you wiped out a *federale* artillery column over in the Baja, too. They say one time five rebel *muchachas* tried for to make you beg for mercy in bed. And they say you wore the five of them out!"

He modestly replied, "That never happened. More than three in a bed ain't practical unless two experiment with . . . sophisticated notions. What does this Toss Turner look like, Miss Ramona? I've heard him described as sort of a cow or dressed like a traveling salesman."

She shrugged closer and said, "When he left, downstairs, was wearing a dark vest over light blue shirt. Dark pants. Gray sombrero with the crown crushed like your own. Wore his gun, a Remington .45 I think, on his right hip, low, with the holster tied to his thigh with latigo thongs. While you and La Mariposa were waiting for that troop train high above the railroad yards, did you take all your clothes off?"

He said he didn't know what she was talking about. She said she sure admired a man who didn't brag about his conquests, even when he had the chance to say he'd

122

made love to the far famed *La Mariposa*. Longarm had thought he'd been doing all right that time in that signal tower down Mexico way. It was enough to give a man a hard-on, just thinking back to how passionate such a pretty little thing could get with the taste of impending disaster in the air.

Folk were funny that way. It likely had something to do with Professor Darwin's theory about evolution. But it sure beat all how horny nurses and wounded men got with the sound of guns in the distance or how rape and blood-shed seemed to run together as if everybody was liquored up.

He knew human nature, as well as his own, to sense the excitement in the dry afternoon air had them both breathing harder than they really needed to and duty had to come before pleasure, dang it, so as Ramona rolled off the bed to kneel on the Navajo rug beside it and grope at the fly of his jeans Longarm told her gently but firmly to cut that out. But his old organ grinder was letting his true feelings show as she hauled it out into the daylight, gasping, "*¡Ay, que tragosas!* What have I gotten myself into, or vice versa?"

Longarm pleaded, "Cut that out, Miss Ramona. Toss Turner's been looking all over town for me, with no luck so far and *la siesta* setting in. If he has a lick of sense he'll come on home and kip-out 'til it cools off outside!"

Ramona never answered. Her mouth was too full as Longarm moaned it just wasn't fair a stiff dick had so little conscience. He begged her to be careful with those teeth as she swallowed his throbbing glans past the base of her tongue. So he warned her it was her own fault if he had to come that fool way and then he saw he wasn't the only man coming at the moment by a long shot!

The cuss down yonder, hugging the shade under a tel-escoped gray Stetson, was wearing a dark vest over a light blue shirt with his six-gun riding low in a tie-down hol-ster. And he was coming fast as Longarm came in Ra-mona's throbbing throat, Lord love the both of 'em!

Chapter 15

The killer who'd given himself the whimsical handle of Toss Turner was footsore and frustrated as he strode his way back to his posada for some cold *cerveza* and a well-earned siesta after running himself ragged in a vain hunt for the elusive Longarm. They'd told him at more than one place he'd asked how he'd just missed the big moose and mayhaps it was just as well. For it would be way easier to slip away in the cool shades of evening if he blew the son of a bitch up after things cooled off.

El Corazon de Trinidad had some cooling to go at the moment and dammit he'd used up the clean shirts he'd brought with him. But mayhaps if he hung the one he had on by the window to air out as he treated himself to a flop it could carry him through or, hell, he had the *dinero* to just up and buy a fresh shirt once things opened up again that evening.

He resisted the impulse to break into a trot as he spied the shady entrance of La Posada de la Junta smiling in welcome ahead. His pals had been on the money when they'd advised him to hole up with Mexicans on the outskirts of town. That jolly widow who ran the place had enough white blood in her to tolerate gringo strangers who paid up front and he'd been too slick to let the greasers know how fluent he was in Spanish. So being smart enough to look dumb he'd heard the help say nothing more treacherous than *gringo chingado* in a casual tone. And that seemed fair. He thought they were a bunch of fucking greasers, too.

The point was that they'd bought his simple tale of being a trail boss for hire, waiting there in Trinidad for a big wind from Texas to blow in with a handsome job offer. Pals who'd stayed with old Ramona Montoya in the past had found her a live-and-let-live landlady not inclined as most to speculate on the past lives of paying customers and, better yet, not in too tight with the Anglo business establishment in those parts.

As he made it to the ever-open doorway, Toss Turner hoped they'd left the bar open in spite of *la siesta*. Pesky Mex traditions could be the price for doing business with fucking greasers. Then he remembered ordering a cold beer from the ice chest the afternoon before and so he was smiling as he stepped into the darker and way cooler interior.

After that things got confounding. What felt like a ton of soft bricks thundered down on him from on high and then something harder collided with his skull behind one ear and then there were all those pretty little stars swirling in the whirlpool of ink he was falling into and then he just felt dreadful for a million years as his world came slowly back together around him.

Once he'd recovered enough to make a lick of sense of things, Longarm's victim found himself seated on the dirt floor of what seemed a root cellar with his wrists handcuffed behind the upright post his spine was braced against. He was missing his hat, his gunbelt and the dynamite bomb he'd had under his sweaty shirt. By the light of a candlestick on the dirt floor betwixt them, Toss Turner saw Longarm was going through his wallet as he hunkered on his haunches.

"No fair! You jumped me from ahint!" Toss Turner

protested with the righteous indignation of the wrongdoer.

Longarm smiled thinly by candlelight to reply, not unkindly, "I don't recall anybody yelling, Duck, here comes a bomb! So I'd say we're even. According to this Denver library card and your voter's registration you answer to the name of Toss N. Turner, you cute little thing. I've been trying in vain to come up with a more sensible title to your unfamiliar features whilst you tossed and turned your way back from the land of Nod. But you're going to have to help me out. Who might you be and how come you keep trying to blow me up with dynamite?"

His captive asked, "I talk and walk? That's the only deal I'll make with you, Longarm. Wouldn't offer *that* if I hadn't been assured you're a man of your word."

Longarm modestly replied, "I'm so pleased to learn you and your murdersome friends thought that much of me. As to whether I'll feel free to let you off the hook in exchange for bigger fish, I'd have to hear your fish story, first."

Toss Turner sullenly replied, "*Chinge tu madre*. What have you got on me that'll stand up in court?"

Longarm cast the fake ID and folding money aside as he fished out a smoke, deciding, "So you're wanted in other parts on charges more serious than mere *attempted* murder and we do have a problem, don't we?"

He broke out a waterproof Mex match to light his cheroot before he continued, "As they likely told you when they paid you to blow me up, I pack a federal badge and have no call to pester state or county lawmen about hearsay unless they up and ask me right out what I might hear. So let's get some cards face-up in the dirt betwixt us. Las Animas County could have you making little rocks out of bigger rock for quite a spell on those two dynamite detonations here in town alone."

Toss Turner snorted, "Prove it! Show me a witness willing to finger me for kicking over a trash can!"

Longarm easily replied, "Don't have to. I ain't the district attorney who no-doubt has many a witness he can recruit on short notice if he has to."

He took a drag on his cheroot, blew a thoughtful smoke ring, and added, "He may not feel he has to. The brand of dynamite and the nails imbedded in the sticks I just removed from your person ought to match what they've gathered at the scenes of your earlier vandalism. On the other hand, like I said, unless you've blown somebody else up more serious and federal . . ."

Toss Turner said, "I know what you want. So here's my opening hand, face up. I'll tell you why I was trying to blow you up and I'll agree not to blow you up no more, in exchange for a twenty-four-hour head start with that wallet and my Remington back. Deal?"

Longarm took another thoughtful drag before he decided, "Got to study on your generous offer. We both know I'd rather have a big fish than a worm like you. On the other hand I'd sure feel silly if it turned out I'd let a worm wanted for blowing up school houses and raping schoolmarms go."

He reached for the candlestick betwixt them and rose to his considerable height with it as he decided, "Why don't we both study on our options a spell? No need to bother your pals or mine 'til later this afternoon. I aim to meet somebody around suppertime in the hopes he'll have come up with some answers. When and where did you say your pals would be expecting to meet up with you this evening?"

Toss Turner snorted, "Nice try, but no cigar. I talk and walk or you can go sit on an egg and see what hatches out of the same."

As Longarm moved toward the stairs the killer handcuffed to the upright added, "Hey, leave that candlestick with this child, Longarm! You can't expect me to sit here in the fucking dark!"

To which Longarm replied in an amiable tone, "Sure

I can. Just watch me. It ain't safe to leave candles burning untended, Toss. So you just sit tight a spell and further along, like the old church song says, we may know more about it."

"This ain't right!" his prisoner protested as Longarm made it over to the stairs. He didn't ask the killer if he was afraid of the dark. Heaps of grown men who were never admitted to it and Longarm didn't want to encourage any lying habits.

He went up the stairs as Toss Turner yelled dreadful things about his poor old mother back home in West-by-God Virginia.

Seeing it had been dug by Mexicans, the root cellar wasn't directly under the kitchen. As Longarm crossed the back garth to rejoin Ramona at her kitchen door the pleasantly plump merry widow asked what happened next. Longarm told her, "He ain't going nowheres and nobody's expecting to meet up with him during *la siesta*. If a few hours listening to things going bump in the dark fails to loosen his tongue I reckon I'll turn him over to my old pal, Detective Caruso, and let them tuck him away under Firehouse Number One for safekeeping."

She said she still had her *pobrecitos* watching all the approaches and suggested she might send one for to fetch the police sooner so nobody at the *posada* would have to worry about him.

Longarm shook his head. He knew she had more than the manpower to fetch anybody. The local Mex economy was conducted on the Hispano-Roman *tradiciónes de patrocinio*. Mexicans with money, like anybody with money, were inclined to pay no more than they had to for anything. On the other hand, unlike that Mister Scrooge made so famous by Mister Dickens, well-to-do Mexicans just hated to watch folk starve to death. So whether they really needed more hired help or not they were inclined to take on the kith or kin of anybody they'd already hired, working them now and again for room and board or mayhaps a few *centavos* on special occasions. So this, rather than inherent sloth, was why you found so many Mexicans doing nothing much for the *patron* or *patrona* they ran occasional errands for.

He told Ramona, "Once I turn that cuss in your root cellar over to any local law I've lost any chance to make him talk. So I'd as soon hang on to him as long as I can without having to really work at it. With a little bit of luck, his pals not knowing where I have him at the moment, one or more might show up here, asking for him."

Longarm grinned wolfishly and added, "It's always easier sweating two or more members of the same gang, separated, not certain what sort of deals anybody else might make."

Ramona gasped, "*¡Ay, mierditas!* How many *ladrones* might we have for to deal with, here?"

He soothed, "I can only hope. I doubt any will show up before dark and by that time I'll have turned him over to my own pals. Even if they should come looking for him, he ain't in his room or anywhere's else they might expect. Tell your help to just act dumb and natural if anybody asks for Toss Turner. I'll do the rest. Playing by ear. So for openers I reckon it might be best if I holed up out of sight for now."

She grinned dirty and said she knew just the place.

Then she led him by the hand into her own chambers behind the bar down one wall of her downstairs tap room.

Idly wondering as he did so why it felt sort of awkward undressing in broad day in front of an already naked lady who'd already sucked him off all the way, Longarm soon discovered that, as he'd hoped, the more than Junoesque Ramona didn't need any pillows under her ample bottom to tilt her old ring-dang-doo at a might welcoming angle as he mounted her with no further ado.

They'd established upstairs she felt it a great honor for to *rabiar* or rage together with *El Brazo Largo* and he knew better than to ask her not to brag about him having sixteen inches and leaving her in a condition requiring surgical attention. He'd already seen, from the expression of pleased surprise on her face as she'd hauled his old organ grinder out that like most other experienced women of a certain age she'd taken a heap of earlier brags about him with a grain of salt.

What passionate *señoritas* said about a man they found exciting wasn't what made *Los Rurales* and other Mex lawmen so anxious to cut his balls off, slit his throat, rip out his guts and then kill him. The stories his *male* Mex admirers spread about a nine foot version of El Cid kicking in El Presidente's palace door and making El Presidente Diaz watch as his wife and daughters were raped in turn, swearing undying love to *El Brazo Largo* as he made them feel like real *mujeres* at last, were what made *Los Rurales* so cross with him.

As he made Ramona feel like she was losing her virginity, she asked if the stories about him and that Mother Superior were true. He soberly assured her he'd only fucked all the pretty nuns in that fool convent, and only them because they'd asked him.

He was afraid she believed him. He was sure she meant to pass it on as part of his growing legend and thanked his lucky stars Reporter Ford of the way skinnier but just as bouncy bottom had been content, so far, to write him up as Denver's answer to Dan'l Boone, Kit Carson, and Wild Bill rolled up in one big winner. Her more prim and proper Anglo readers were more interested, or felt less tittersome, about blood and gore. Schoolkids were encouraged to memorize "The Charge of the Light Brigade." But whilst it was all right to dwell on six hundred horses and riders being torn to bloody shreds by shot and shell they'd put you in jail for selling them a copy of the *Kama Sutra*, advising folk how to *pleasure* one another.

Old Ramona, bless her widowed heart, didn't need Hindu contortions to pleasure herself or any man. She just provided a continued rolling earthquake or in her case ass-quake for him to ride out with her hot man-hole clamped tight as the teen-aged cherry she kept telling Longarm he had her harkening back to.

When a man closed his eyes and harkened some, himself, she surely did recall him to that big old Susie Conners on that hayride under a harvest moon that time. Susie had begged him to shut his eyes when she'd let him shove her shift above her mighty mature tits and she'd smelled more of lavender water than the musky sandalwood perfume Ramona was wearing and, by damn, it sure got exciting when a man opened his eyes as he was fixing to come in a pleasantly plump dishwater blonde to find himself coming in a downright delightfully built dusky brunette.

So when Ramona wanted to get on top he let her and it sure beat all how a gal that big could slide up and down his inspired erection like a kid on a merry-go-round horse with her head thrown back and her long black hair whipping every direction but off.

They were well established sex partners by the end of *la siesta*, having had the time and taken the time to come up with some mighty novel positions with time out for pillow talk and shared tobacco. So he found his fool self agreeing with Ramona when she said she was glad nobody had come looking for that *pendejo* in her root cellar.

But that reminded him Toss Turner was still there. So he told Ramona where to get in touch with him if anybody did come by for Toss Turner and by then they'd fornicated so thoroughly she was satisfied with a kiss and a feel once he'd hauled on his duds, boots, and six-gun.

Back in the root cellar, Longarm struck a wax-stemmed waterproof match to see his prisoner still there, seated in a patch of mud around that upright. Toss Turner spat, "You inhuman hell fiend! You up and abandoned me with no way to even unbutton my fly and look how I've pissed myself!"

Longarm said, "I sent a *muchacho* over to Firehouse

Number One to fetch us a paddy wagon. So your pals won't see you've pissed yourself as we pass by. They won't even know where we're holding you and we'll likely manage to hold you at least seventy-two hours on suspicion before you're booked on at least malicious mischief. Of course, if you'd care to tell me who you've been working for . . ."

"I talk and walk or you can fuck your mother and her mother's mother all the way back to Mother Eve!" the literally pissed prisoner hissed.

So Longarm went back upstairs to wait for the paddy wagon, seeing the son of a bitch seemed such an old hand at their game.

Chapter 16

Once he had Toss Turner lodged in the cellar of Firehouse Number One and those handcuffs back where they usually rode on his gunbelt, Longarm ambled on over to the Harvey House, seeing it was almost time to meet old Gilchrist there.

But the section security supervisor was waiting in the doorway for him and as Longarm approached Gilchrist called out, "Change of plans. I got to carry you home to my house for a real set-down supper unless I mean to sleep on the sofa tonight. That's my surrey up the walk. Let's go."

Longarm fell in step with the older man, even as he protested he'd been fixing to grab a quick bite in the Harvey House.

Gilchrist proved how well he supervised his section by saying, "That pretty Jew gal you've been out to get fired ain't on duty this evening. I made the mistake of dropping by my place, earlier, to tell the wife and a visiting niece I might grab a bite at the Harvey House as well. Did you know they've run yarns about you as far east as Iowa, you town-taming cuss?"

Longarm sighed and said, "I've asked them to cut that out. Old James Butler Hickok might still be alive if Ned

133

Buntline hadn't built him up as such a worthy target for asshole punks like Cockeyed Jack McCall. Who's out to shoot me in the back, your wife or your visitor from Iowa?"

As Gilchrist untethered his matching mules from the hitch rail in front of the station he said, "Neither, as far as they'll own up to. My wife's niece, Prudence, is visiting us with her two kids, Elroy and Iris. *They* were the ones who begged for you like candy. Elroy is old enough to read blood and thunder and little Iris seems to think you must be an Indian. I told her you weren't. But she said she'd never heard tell of anybody but Indians having names like Rain In The Face, Yellow Hand or Long Arm."

As they got in, Gilchrist added, "Their elders and me agreed it would be easier to just carry you on home and we're having this right interesting Dutch shit the womenfolk put their pretty heads together for. My wife's family were Pennsylvania Dutch before they wound up in Iowa. They call what we're having something like sore bragging and it's served with potato dumplings."

Longarm said, "I suspect *sauerbraten* might be how you say it. Had some at this beer garden in Denver and you've sold me on your home cooking. You start with a prime roast and let it soak a while in sweet-pickle brine. I was wondering if you'd heard anything solid about that money train you made mention of."

As they trotted south along Commercial Street Gilchrist smiled sheepishly and said, "I was hoping you'd forgotten that. There ain't no money train in particular coming down from Denver tomorrow. More than one D&RG combination worth robbing instead of a blamed milk train. But it seems the different banks draw separate from the Denver Mint as their needs require. So no target in particular will be more tempting in the cold gray dawn to come and they *said* they aimed to hit again this coming *weekend*!"

Longarm filled the railroad dick in on his arrest of Toss Turner whilst he drove south along what had recently been the Goodnight Cattle Trail, now lined to either side with serious to frilly shops and such.

The railroad dick said neither the obvious alias nor the way better description Longarm offered added up to anybody he'd seen on any recent Wanted fliers. Gilchrist decided, "That has to be the professional name of a man who hires out as a demolitions hairpin. A section hand good with his dukes may be content with the name they sprinkled him. But a boxer putting up his dukes for prize money is inclined to call himself Knuckles, Rocky, Jumping Jack, and such. I think you're correct in assuming he threw dynamite your way, more than once, as directed by somebody who knows you better. Is it safe to assume Detective Caruso is working on that bay pony Turner was riding when he tossed that first bomb in Nuevo Trinidad?"

Longarm said, "He is. We naturally asked Toss Turner but he can't seem to get it through his head that you catch more flies with honey than with vinegar. Town law would have treated him to a change of pants and a shower had he been less surly with his answers. I wonder what he's so worried we might find out, or guess at, soon as he stops playing *tu madre* with us."

By the time they'd driven as far as Fifth Street the business structures had given way to private homes with vacant lots to spare along the west side of Commercial. Longarm had already noticed most of the old-time Spanish 'dobes were closer to the river and strung out eastwards from that Santa Trinidad church. You saw some Mex faces the way they were headed. You saw some Mex faces no matter where you headed around Trinidad. But when they got to Gilchrist's place it was a whitewashed frame farmhouse one might see in Iowa, transplanted to a five acre awkwardness too small to farm and too big for one family to manage without hired help.

So Longarm wasn't surprised when some Mex or more

likely Tanoan kid came out of the carriage house to take charge of the team. But when he followed Gilchrist inside he found the lady of the house presiding over her kitchen with nobody helping her but a pretty little waif who looked too young and helpless to be the mother of the boy and girl jumping up and down as they asked Uncle Warren where Longarm was.

The motherly but not-bad Charity Gilchrist née Dorfmann shooed everyone out on the front porch to work it out whilst she and her niece, Prudence, got supper ready.

Longarm sat on the steps and held off on lighting up as the two kids from Iowa sat on either side of him, with Elroy more willing to believe in Longarm than his little sister, once he'd asked to hold Longarm's big .44-40 and been politely but firmly denied the opportunity to kill himself or anyone else.

On the far side, the four- or five-year-old Iris demanded to know why neither he nor that other Indian, Billy Dancing Corn, wore feathers or war paint.

Elroy snorted, "Longarm ain't no Indian, you dumb girl. He's a cowboy and I don't think much of Billy Dancing Corn as Indians go. He told me I was full of it when I showed him the arrowhead I found, and what kind of Indian don't know Indians used to make arrowheads out of stone? You want to see my arrowhead, Uncle Longarm?"

When Longarm allowed he sure would the kid from Iowa produced a sharp pebble he said he'd found out back cultivatin' corn for Aunt Charity. As Longarm gravely examined the round pebble some steel-shod hoof had cracked in two, his host, Gilchrist, explained his wife had put the kids to chores to keep them out of trouble whilst out from underfoot.

Longarm said, "Well, it might have been some old-timer's *start* at an arrowhead, Elroy. This lady I know at a museum in Denver says they doubt any particular cave man ever woke up one morning to decide he might as well start the so-called Stone Age. Folk with no better tools just used any sticks or rocks they found as best they could until somebody here and another yonder saw you could get a stick or rock to work better if you changed it's *shape* a mite. This museum lady I mentioned told me they've found old-time Stone Age tools or weapons ranging from little more than a pebble with one sharp edge, such as this one, to finely crafted knife blades, ax heads, spear points, and arrowheads, of course."

Gilchrist chimed in, not unkindly but sort of smugly to Longarm's way of thinking, "You kids got out our way far too late for hunting stone arrowheads, Elroy. Indians started trading skins for *iron* arrowheads way back when and all this land's been settled by more civilized folk over a hundred years, now."

Elroy's lower lip trembled but he managed a brave face as he tried, "Must have been Indians out here before there was anybody else! Ain't that true, Uncle Longarm?"

Their supper visitor allowed that seemed reasonable, but suggested they leave the question open until such time as they might have a tad more evidence, pro or con.

Miss Prudence came out to tell them all it was time to wash up for supper. So they all went out back to do so, at the pump by the kitchen door. Some of them naturally went further, without comment.

Queen Victoria had gotten to set the moral standards of her era with advantages denied the general public. Growing up in well-staffed palaces, she'd no doubt found it possible to take a standing shit in a hoop skirt and just walk on, knowing her devoted servants would stoop and scoop before anybody noticed and, after that, she'd had the scientific plumbing of Mister Crapper at her disposal behind closed doors.

The point was that nobody in late Victorian times was supposed to know human beings as well as other critters *had* to shit and piss on occasion.

So the less scientific but no less proper late Victorians had learned not to *notice* such matters. In a world run on steam and horse power the ladies too proper to admit a table had *legs* could carry on delicate as ever in a carriage as the horse taking them to or fro lifted its tail to fart and shit a dozen apples. When they had to take a shit *themselves*, nobody seemed to notice as they picked their dainty way to the outhouse set in most backyards under its own cloud of flies. By mutual covert treaty, nobody old enough to manage without help ever excused themselves to go to the outhouse. They just got up and went, with nobody expecting to be invited back again asking them where they were headed or where they might have been. So nobody asked where Longarm was headed when he took a stroll across the backyard, took a long leak down one of the holes and dropped a scoop of the limed dirt provided down into the darkness after it. Nobody was looking his way as he mosied back by way of the kitchen garth along the sunny north fence line. Nobody commented when he was last to make it inside.

He saw they'd made room for their Indian hand at the kitchen table and dug in to the *sauerbraten* old Gilchrist had bragged on. The potato dumplings and salsify or oyster roots served with it were good as well. Salsify was one of the few vegetables Longarm managed to enjoy some. It looked like pale waxy carrots and didn't really taste so much like oysters. Folk who couldn't figure out *what* salsify tasted like had decided on oysters, the way they said rattlesnake tasted like chicken. He was the only one there to comment on the salsify. So they likely grew some out back. He wasn't sure what the *tops* of salsify looked like. He was sure they'd drilled in some sweet corn, onions, and peppers.

Being everyone there had been raised country, nobody talked like society folk whilst grubbing, and the dessert was a choke-cherry pie, baked with a lot of white sugar, of course, and served with rat trap cheese. Longarm wasn't lying when he told the ladies he hadn't had a meal that good since a birthday party in Denver.

138

The days getting longer, and the Gilchrists keeping country hours it was still daylight outside as Billy Dancing Corn helped the womenfolk with the dishes, the kids went out back to play before bedtime and the two lawmen smoked on the front porch to jaw some more about those milk train robberies as the sun was working its way down behind the Sangre de Cristos. It was just as well they had full bellies and good tobacco comforting them as they talked in tedious circles.

Since he was not in fact a sworn-in lawman but a glorified railyard bull who'd worked his way up from tossing bums off freight cars, Gilchrist felt the way to question the mysterious Toss Turner involved brass knuckles if not hot pokers.

Longarm shook his head and said, "You do get *sudden* answers that way. You don't always get the *truth* out of folk that way. Back in the days of that Spanish Inquisition, they got scared human beings to confess they flew through the sky to fornicate with mighty unlikely looking imps of Satan. I find it tough to buy *all* them old women in Salem Village sucking off a jet black demon with an ice-cold prick as hard as steel, too. I already put some *reasonable* pressure on that bomb-throwing cuss who wants us to call him Toss. He's smart enough to hold out for *carte blanche* and human enough to accuse most anyone on earth if we twist his arm. Caruso agrees our best bet would be finding out who in thunder he really is, seeing how bad he might be wanted, by whom, and offering him a lesser local charge to answer for. He already knows Las Animas County can't hang more than a year on him for anything we can prove without his help."

Gilchrist snorted, "Come on! Didn't he kill that *horse* with an infernal machine and ain't that a hanging offense here in Colorado?"

Longarm shook his head to say, "*Stealing* a horse can still get a man hung out this way. They've never taken that one off the books but they don't enforce it often and

139

any lawyer worth his salt would surely argue there's not one word about *murdering* a horse on the books. Can't even prove he attempted to murder *me* if his lawyer sells one juror the notion he was just being boistersome."

There came some whooping and hollering from inside and then young Elroy busted out on the porch to yell, "Look what me and Iris just now found in the kitchen garth!"

His little sister came out to join them as Elroy displayed the white agate arrowhead he'd spotted amid the radish tops. Little Iris had found another knapped from red chert.

Warren Gilchrist took the white one to hold up to the sunset light as he marveled, "Danged if this *don't* look like an arrowhead! What do you make of it, Longarm?"

Longarm held the one Elroy offered for inspection up to soberly declare, "Looks like an arrowhead to me. You say you found this in that same garden dirt, Elroy?"

The kid said he surely had. Then he said he meant to find some more and lit out on them with his little sister bawling after him. Longarm managed to keep a sober face as the older man he was smoking with muttered about living and learning.

Longarm agreed you never wanted to take anything for granted. He'd been a kid one time and his elders had laughed at *his* imaginings, too.

The two women came out to join them. The sparrow-boned but not too bad Prudence Whatever allowed the sunset was divine as she sat on the steps not too close but not all that far from Longarm. Discussions about milk trains were dropped as they all agreed about that sunset until the sun had gone and set. As the sky to the west went from scarlet to ruby Charity Gilchrist nudged her man and said something about needing help inside. As he followed her in Warren Gilchrist murmured to his woman, "I don't know about this, Charity. That federal man is a pal and we're working on the same case but . . . I've been

140

given to understand he's a bit of a rogue with the ladies!"

To which the motherly Charity demurely replied, "Oh, let's *hope* so. My poor little niece hasn't even held hands with a man since she left that awful drunk she married as an innocent child!"

Chapter 17

Back out on the porch steps, in the gathering dusk, Prudence Fisher, as her married name panned out, proved somewhat sharper than most men took her for at first glance.

That wasn't hard. At first glance she looked country. Longarm was better with kids than with women who didn't look full grown. But it would have been rude to head back to *La Posada de la Junta* and more grown-up surroundings that early. Some older neighborhood kids were still playing "Kick the Can" down the street. He figured he'd light another cheroot on his way back to old Ramona in say another half hour or so.

Prudence broke their friendly enough silence by asking, "How did you ever *do* that, with the arrowheads, Custis? I saw you dropping something in the kitchen garth on your way . . . back to the house. It was awfully sweet of you. But how could you have known a boy you'd never met would be hunting for arrowheads in a yard you'd never visited before?"

He didn't ask how come she'd been watching a man she'd only just met traipsing back and forth from the outhouse. He said magicians weren't supposed to give away their secrets. When she swore she'd never let her kids in on it Longarm explained, "Pure luck. I'd been carrying a handful of tourist souvenirs around with a view to getting rid of it somewheres. Your Elroy's budding career in archaeology offered the chance to kill two birds with the same stone arrowheads."

She laughed, said it had still been awfully sweet, and asked him how on earth he'd ever wound up with a pocket full of such nonsense.

After he'd explained about the old Indian at the railroad station she moved closer to declare, "My Aunt Charity was right about you not being half as wicked as some say! Neither my Elroy nor that poor old drunken Indian were sassy things you were out to flirt with. You were just being *nice* to them!"

Longarm said, "Aw, mush, the whole deal set me back less than a dollar and who said anything about that old Tanoan being drunk? I only took him for a street merchant out to make an honest living, such as it may be."

She looked away in the tricky light and murmured, "You're right. That was not a charitable thing to say about a man I'd never met. I fear I've been . . . taught to feel suspicious about anybody living closer to the edge than the rest of us. You see, the man I married had a drinking problem and couldn't seem to hold a job."

Longarm grimaced and replied, "No offense, Miss Prudence, but once you say you married a drunk you've told the whole story to anyone who's heard it before. It's always the same story and if it's any comfort, men who've married women who can't handle liquor tell much the same sad tale."

She sighed and said, "I know. I've talked to other grass widows about the drunks they finally gave up on. We all tell the same round-robin of childish spats, tender nights of making up and swearing off, followed by yet more childish spats, lame excuses, raging demands for undeserved respect and so on, 'til it's time to pack it in or lay down and die."

143

Longarm said, "You did the right thing for your kids and yourself. As a lawman I've been there and it can really get messy. Bad enough when a drunk just kills his or herself. Sometimes they crave company."

It was too dark to be certain. But she sounded as if she was crying quietly when she said, "I left after he'd beaten me, twice, in front of the children. I think he scared them more than he scared me. He beat me when I refused to hit up Aunt Charity and Uncle Warren for more drinking money. Kind neighbors took us in and hid us until the dear folk inside sent us enough to join them out here. A lawyer Uncle Warren works with has filed for my divorce from Elroy Senior. So I'll soon be free to start over and . . . Custis, I'm scared. I don't know *how* to start over!"

He shrugged and suggested, "You just let nature take its course, Miss Prudence. You're a handsome young woman, no offense, and there's not too many women of any description out this way. Just bide your time. Let word get around that you're free, and just take you pick from all the swains who come calling."

She said, "You sound like Aunt Charity. She just laughs when I tell her I don't know how to . . . well, set and spark with a man in the dark like this."

He said she seemed to be doing all right, so far.

She said, "Silly, we're not sparking. We're just talking. I mean I've never . . . you know, held hands and swapped spit with a man I've never . . . known in the biblical sense."

She covered her face with her skirt and blurted, "Oh, Lord, this is so awkward! Whatever must you think of me?"

He said, "I think I see what your problem might be. You married up young, whilst other gals your age were still holding hands and swapping spit as they made up their minds. You wound up going all the way with the first man who ever gave you a warm kiss and some naughty grabbing, right?"

She sobbed, "I never let him feel me up before we were man and wife in the eyes of the Lord. The first time he ever . . . touched my breast was after he'd deflowered me and if only he hadn't been so weak-natured about drinking I'd have been in heaven! I *like* what it feels like with a man in bed. But what do men think of any woman who can't hold out one night after they let a man kiss them riding home from a church social in a buggy?"

Longarm said, "Warm natured. But you're right about that being rough on a grass widow's reputation. She's already got two strikes against her as a woman known to have had some experience in such matters. Unless she can hold things down to say a kiss goodnight at the front door she's not likely to attract the sort of swain I assume you're interested in."

She took one of his hands in both of her own as she told him he was so understanding. She said, "I've been wondering how, oh how, an unworldly country girl with two children might learn to just . . . you know, without getting too hot to hold out for honorable intentions!"

He gravely assured her, "You have to learn to pretend. Once the loaf has been cut it's hard as anything to keep from offering another slice. But if you set your mind to it you can control such passions by gritting you teeth and just saying no."

She asked if he didn't find it nigh impossible to say no, once the desires came over him.

He soberly replied, "Matter of fact I just this afternoon felt torn by such conflicting desires. We have to be strong when it just ain't the right time to give in."

She said, "I've never in my life kissed a man, alone in the dark, without it leading to something more. I used to swear I'd never let my brute of a husband touch me that way again and yet, when he did, I just couldn't refuse him what we both wanted."

He didn't have a sensible answer for that. So he didn't offer one.

She timidy asked, "Would you . . . help me see what it feels like to . . . kiss *pure*, Custis?"

He laughed lightly and replied, "That sure seems a novel suggestion, Miss Prudence. But like the old maid said when she kissed the clock, I reckon I ought to try everything, once!"

So he took her in his arms and kissed her, hardly pure, albeit it had been her idea to stick her tongue in his mouth like that. As they came up for air she gasped, "Oh, dear Lord! Let's go across the road and fuck in those bushes!"

To which Longarm gravely replied, "That ain't really what you want us to do, Miss Prudence. You want to learn how to kiss *pure*. So let's try it some more with your pretty pink tongue not so sassy."

They kissed again. Not as French. She still tried to get his free hand under her skirts. But after they'd kissed a few more times she said she was getting the hang of just kissing for pleasure. So he decided it was time to quit whilst they were ahead.

As he got to his feet, Prudence rose with him to walk him arm-and-arm out to the road. When they kissed there like spooners parting for the night she flustered, "Oh, my, this does feel awfully *romantic*, Custis! I never had a man just kiss me goodnight and walk away without . . . you know, before!"

He kissed her on the forehead, wished her good hunting, and lit out to the east with the serious erection all that kid stuff had inspired. He knew he'd have likely acted like a kid back there if good old Ramona hadn't been so good to him, earlier. By the time he'd legged it all the way to her posada on the opposite outskirts of town he was ready to be good to her some more. Trudging through dark streets, idly wondering what might be going on behind all those lamplit window curtains whilst one pictured robust dusky brunettes and waiflike brown-haired gals with not a stitch betwixt them and your dirty imagination could put any man in a mood to do right by a pal.

When he got there, Ramona was delighted to see him but said nobody had been by asking for Toss Turner. He said he didn't care. So they went to her quarters to get out of their awkward vertical positions and, Jesus H. Christ if it didn't feel grand to picture little Prudence taking it to the roots like that as he shut his eyes on top of Ramona.

After that the tawny naked charms of Ramona were worth enjoying in their own right and Longarm had experienced enough charms of various shades, shapes and sizes to rate Ramona well above average. So a good time was had by all as they both measured one another by past times good or bad, and that was about the best thing that could be said for tumbleweeding through a sometimes lonesome world alone.

Having spent more time alone of late, Ramona asked, as they shared a smoke and a cuddle during a breather, whether she could count on him for breakfast. He patted her tawny rump to reply, "Sure would like to spend the whole night here. Can't. Got to be back at my hotel no later than say two A.M. so's they can roust me out for some riding if those tomfools stop that milk train coming up out of New Mexico in the wee small hours."

She pouted he'd only come by for to see if anyone had come calling on Toss Turner, not for to fuck her.

"That's not true!" he lied. "It's commencing to look as if the gang has been following the tactics of the James-Younger Gang and that's another thing to study on."

She didn't know what he was talking about.

He explained, "Before their disastersome Northfield raid just about put the James Boys out of business and exposed their slick hit-and-run ways, they'd confounded lawmen hunting a gang of a dozen or so by *spreading out* betwixt jobs and moving in on a target solo or mayhaps by twos. They dwelt apart and dressed different 'til the day they moved in, with travel dusters or rain slickers over the various duds they had on. Then all of a sudden

147

this gang in identical outfits would stop a train or coach, rob a bank or whatever and ride off in a bunch to be described by witnesses."

He took a drag on their shared cheroot, placed it betwixt her lips, and continued, "Soon as they were out of sight they'd scatter, shuck those identical slickers, and turn in to a rider hither, two riders yon, dressed all sorts of ways and riding sedately in all directions, sometimes offering helpful suggestions as the posse thundered by."

She said, "*Que furtivo. Pero* how did they get caught if they were so clever?"

He said, "Your luck can run out no matter how clever you think you are. As they were gathering by ones and twos to rob the Northfield Bank one of 'em was recognized by a townsman, who spread the word, and as they came out of the bank they were greeted by a fusilade. The hardware man right across the street had been handing out hunting rifles. The Miller Boys were killed, the Younger Boys were captured, they think Frank James may be in Kentucky and Jesse's been spotted now and again in Missouri. The point I'm making is that they ain't holed up in one *posada* and they only get in touch when they have something important to say. Toss Turner was staying here alone. The others, we figure at least five, all told, must be holed up in other parts of Trinidad, north or south of the river. If they know we have Toss Turner locked up they'll never come near his last known address. If they don't know it, yet, they'll have no reason to 'til they're ready to make another daring raid on the morning milk train."

She passed the smoke back to ask in a worried tone, "But then they may come here for to see why he is missing, no?"

He said, "No. These birds are working overtime to *avoid* traps. They're as likely to lay low or, worse yet, scatter, if they think we have one of 'em on ice. Either way, you're not likely to have further dealing with the bunch and, say, have you ever tried it sideways with one thigh draped over and the other down straight?"

She said she hadn't, of course, and he of course pretended to believe there could be a position a lusty widow of a certain age had never tried.

So they were really enjoying one another's company as, meanwhile, over at all-night Harvey House, seated at a corner table betwixt trains, three men dressed nothing at all like cowhands were comparing notes in worried tones.

The one reporting in didn't speak High Dutch for shit. So the boss was softly speaking English as he asked him to go back over what he'd just reported, damn it.

The tail they'd put on Longarm, earlier, insisted, "If I knew how he did it I'd know where the fuck he is right now, Uncle Greg. I followed on foot as that railroad dick he met right here drove down Commercial at a pace I had a time keeping up with. They stopped at his house just as I was fixing to give up with a stitch in my side. I found a corner grocery a furlong off across an open lot and flirted with a fat old gal, drinking soda pop and nibbling crackers until it got dark enough for me to creep in closer. I took a stand in some bushes across from the Gilchrist place. I stood there pissing now and again but too smart to smoke as that infernal Longarm spooned with one of the gals who live there. She must have said no because after a while the two of them came out to the road and I saw them kissing goodnight, outlined by lamplight from the house behind 'em."

Uncle Greg said, "Then what? Step by step!"

The younger sneak said, "Then nothing. Longarm headed back up Commercial as if making for his hotel near Main. I crossed the street to trail from the far side. Commercial was nigh deserted at that hour, that far south, so I hung back about a discreet furlong."

"In the dark of the moon, you owl-eyed wonder?" asked Uncle Greg.

The object of his displeasure looked across the table

149

with the expression of a pup who'd just pissed the rug as he confessed, "I sure *thought* I was tailing him close enough. From time to time he'd pass in front of a lamplit window and there was nobody else moving at that pace over yonder 'til, all of a sudden, he just wasn't there! He must have ducked into one of the places I thought he was passing, Uncle Greg!"

"Or around a corner and along a side street, you fool kid!" the older and more experienced outlaw decided. He shot a glance at the third man there, who tersely replied, "Don't look at *me*. It's after midnight and I was staked out in the lobby of his hotel at sundown. He never came home from wherever he's gone. I don't like this at all, Uncle Greg. We are supposed to be confusing everybody. Where does it say Longarm gets to confuse *us*?"

Chapter 18

Longarm had Main Street all to himself as he walked back to his hotel in the wee small hours, cussing his own weak nature as he considered how that milk train would already be rolling north by now. But knowing the odds on ever having that much free time to spend with good old Ramona again had inspired him to exhaustive efforts and he'd about covered the six furlongs or more to his hotel by the time he was steady on his feet once more.

The night clerk had no messages for him. So Longarm tottered upstairs to see he'd had no sneaky visitors, treated himself to a quick whore bath and flopped bare ass in bed, certain he would never in this life experience another hard-on.

If anybody wanted him they knew where to find him. If they didn't want him he didn't care. He'd never noticed all those rubies embedded in the red sandstone of the Sangre de Cristos before. As he rode through a narrow canyon on that lavender pony off the merry-go-round at the Omaha State Fair he felt tempted to dismount and gather at least a saddlebag of the valuable gems. For a man with a saddlebag of rubies would never have to work again but what if those outlaws got away with all that milk? What would all the little kids in Trinidad drink and what would the poor Widow Fenton do for a living if she had no milk for her dairy and how come Ruth Fenton was candling eggs that morning up a ruby line box canyon, naked as a jay?

Then somebody farther off was cracking a bull whip and threatening to sell somebody for dog food if they didn't dammit *pull* and Longarm opened his eyes to see it was broad-ass daylight, according to the pressed tin ceiling up yonder. He lay slugabed, glad he wasn't part of the morning rush outside as whips cracked, teamsters cussed and somewhere a dog was yipping as if it had been run over. But closing one's eyes didn't work when your empty gut was growling. So he muttered, "Aw, shit, another day, another dollar and what are *you* doing up at this hour, old son?"

His piss hard-on didn't answer. Longarm laughed, got up to drain his bladder, then washed the gum from his eyes and took the time to shave, seeing he seemed to have it. They'd have surely told him had another milk train been stopped. So now it was Thursday and it was starting to look as if they meant to keep that promise about the Friday milk deliveries after all.

"It makes no sense!" Longarm told himself as he razored lather and stubble against the grain in his birthday suit. He took his time and did it righter than usual before he got dressed, treated himself to a breakfast of fried eggs over chili con carne over sliced ham in the hotel dining room and ambled up to Firehouse Number One to see how Toss Turner felt about sharing some information, now.

As he mounted the stairs to approach the desk sergeant he heard the familiar voice of Detective Caruso raging like Mister Hamlet having one of his more emotional moments. As Longarm joined them, the dumpy detective turned to him with the expression of an old maid who'd just been pinched on the ass to yell, "It's insane! I can't believe it! I won't have it! These cocksucking excuses for bumbling idiots have let Toss Turner out on bail! What

152

the fuck am I doing on a force run by bare-faced crooks when I could be out selling brooms door to door!"

The desk sergeant protested, "Watch who you're calling a crook, you fat dago know-it-all! I wasn't on duty when that greasy lawyer showed up in the wee small hours with that bondsman from Courthouse Square. All I know is that my blotter has Toss Turner out on a thousand-dollar bail as of four A.M. The night sergeant *asked* who'd put up that sort of money for a noisy vagrant. They declined to answer and the law books say they were within their rights."

Caruso told Longarm before he was asked, "Turner was being held on a thousand-dollars' bail by order of a judge I'd mistaken for an honest man!"

Longarm said, "Thousand dollars sounds about right. The framers of our constitution, in their infinite wisdom, said every accused felon had the right to a reasonable bail and the worse thing we had on Turner for sure was that dead livery nag."

"What'll you bet he jumps bail and we never see him again?" asked the outraged local lawman.

Longarm said, "If you're right, that'll mean somebody with mighty deep pockets wanted him out of jail mighty bad. Meanwhile neither one of us could arrest him if we could find him, before the date set for . . . ah, Sergeant?"

The desk sergeant consulted his blotter to reply. "He's to appear for pre-trial the middle of next month."

Longarm swore under his breath and said, "There you go. Nobody can touch him until then unless he tosses another bomb and I'll be surprised as hell if I'm still in town for his hearing. But what the hell, you got two property managers and the owner of that poor horse to press charges if he's still in town."

Caruso asked, "What if he's not in town?"

Longarm replied, "I just said that. It's starting to look to me as if somebody with a whole lot of money to invest in my demise sent a paid killer in to blow me up. The

153

one so anxious to see the last of me must have promised to get Turner off if he was caught, provided and only provided he didn't spill any beans. Turner kept his end of the bargain. So now he's out on bail and likely long gone."

He reached for a smoke as he thoughtfully added, "You'd know better than me how to get local lawyers and bondsmen to offer a hint as to who made Turner's bail."

Caruso shook his head morosely to reply, "I know we're talking about a lawyer slimy as the bottom of a spittoon and bail bondsmen have the same council-client rights to privacy. Sometimes I'm dead certain the laws of this country are written by totally crooked lawyers!"

Longarm gently pointed out, "Totally crooked lawyer is a redundancy. Professor Darwin's theory of evolution explains how the fittest, or the ones who win the most cases, survive. Anything new on milk trains, Pard?"

Caruso said, "I understand the sheriff's department is working on that bullshit with the railroads. Both of them. This railroad dick has his own theory about them planning to rob the Denver & Rio Grande for real money after getting everyone to guard the morning milk along the Santa Fe line."

It would have slowed Longarm down to go into his conversations about money trains with old Gilchrist. So he said he'd see what they had to say over at the county courthouse and they parted friendly.

Nothing in Trinidad was all that far from anything else. But he was beginning to feel like that merry-go-round pony by the time he got to the cluster of whitewashed frame county facilities they were using as they bought-out a more serious center closer to Maple Street. Towns west of the big muddy seemed to have a tough time deciding on their exact shape from one day to the next.

At the courthouse they told him the Judge Hecht who'd set Turner's bail was up in Denver at a political gathering. At the sheriff's department he was told the sheriff was in

Denver at the same meeting and nobody had stopped the milk train that morning. The undersheriff Longarm spoke with said those desperados were really fixing to get it if they hit the next morning as they'd promised. Railroad dicks as well as county law would be posted every few miles along the tracks in numbers to more than cope with the usual quartet.

When Longarm said he had reason to expect at least five riders, now, the county lawman allowed a dozen or more would still be in trouble.

Lawyers were nigh impossible to talk to even when they weren't slimy. Hoping to have better luck with that bail bondsman, Longarm figured he'd walked to first base after two strikes and just one important ball.

The bondsman who worked out of the back of a tailor shop across from the county jail refused to say who might have gotten his client's bail. He refused to say how much security Turner's pal or pals had put up. Longarm got nowhere asking if Turner had even offered an address to write to if he should fail to show up for his hearing. But the slippery member of the courthouse gang slipped up by never turning a hair when Longarm promised him flat out that nobody called Toss Turner was about to show up for any hearing in the near or distant future.

The older, fatter, and balder bondsman just shrugged when Longarm told him, "Let me count the ways he adds up to a paid assassin no doubt wanted in other parts for more than *attempted* murder. Nobody ever named any kid Toss Turner. He never hired that livery nag he was seen on that time as Toss Anything. In sum you just posted a thousand dollars bond for a man who never was and never will be if he has a brain in his head. So when he fails to show the county keeps all the money you put up and what makes you so trusting?"

The bondsman just shrugged and said he never discussed his clients.

Longarm was too smart to say what that attitude told

him. He thanked the bucket of lard for his time and left, lighting a cheroot on his way out to congratulate himself.

For he knew, now, the client of Toss Turner who'd gone his bail had put up the whole thousand dollars along with enough extra to make it worth the bondsman's while. Say at least an extra hundred in profit and even more as hush money. The bondsman would have had no call to piss off any lawman unless somebody richer had paid him to.

Ergo what? Some asshole who stopped milk trains for fun but no profit had been willing to spring for say fifteen hundred dollars to bail Turner out and . . . Turner would be long gone by now and if they still meant to kill him, Longarm knew they'd send someone *else* in. Now that he knew Toss Turner on sight they'd be risking a fair fight against that bomb-tossing son of a bitch and if there was one thing certain about this case, it had to be that nobody was fighting *fair*!

And so his morning went as Longarm merry-go-rounded the compact center of Trinidad, old and new. Along about noon someone yoo-hooed him across Main Street, where he jawed a spell with Charity Gilchrist and her niece, Miss Prudence, in the doorway of a ladies notions shop. Prudence told him Billy Dancing Corn had found yet another arrowhead out back and given it to her Elroy like a sport, allowing he'd been wrong about the Shining Times of his people on this slope of the Sangre de Cristos. Longarm was pleased to see she hadn't even told her aunt how those ancient relics might have wound up out back. From the way she was smiling, old Prudence was starting to feel more comfortable out this way.

They parted friendly and Longarm bought a hot tamale and a bottle of cold beer off an old Mex with a pushcart on the corner of Maple and Main.

Closer to his hotel he picked up a morning edition of their *Chronicle News* and yesterday's *Denver Post* to scan through whilst he avoided the noonday sun up in his hired room.

As he entered the Trinidad House's classic cast-iron entrance a she-male figure rose like Venus from the waves, or in this case a tufted leather lobby chair, to head him off on his way upstairs.

It was Elsbeth Ferguson, the redheaded chaperone of those Harvey gals, out of uniform in a becoming summerweight frock of ecru shantung under a straw boater with artificial flowers sprouting from the same.

She said, "I was so afraid I'd have to leave before you returned, Deputy Long. It's about those mysterious Dutchmen loitering about the Harvey House between trains! They have all our girls so frightened!"

Longarm said, "Call me Custis and let's talk about it upstairs, Miss Elsbeth."

Along the way she asked him to call her Beth and explained how Judy Gross hadn't been there to translate as the mystery men had jabbered in Dutch at one another again that very morning.

As Longarm checked the bottom hinge, unlocked the door and ushered her in, the only slightly older chaperone said, "We suspect they must be using our restaurant for secret meetings, but we don't see why. It's true the place is nearly empty for hours at a time. But wouldn't they feel even safer meeting up in some hotel room, such as this one?"

As he shut the door and waved her to a seat on the recently remade bed, bless that colored maid's heart, Longarm replied, "Not if they're staying at different hotels, posadas, rooming houses, and such across town. We figure they're hiring nondescript livery stock at scattered stables, each giving a different story as he leaves his deposit to ride off for a day or so. If you and Miss Judy hadn't brung it to my attention I'd have never thought of a Harvey House for secret meetings. But as soon as you study on it, a restaurant open round the clock but nigh

157

deserted when no trains are stopped outside does seem safer by far than a saloon or . . . house of ill repute."

She looked away, flustered, as Longarm dug into his saddle bags draped over the foot of the bed for the fixings, saying, "I'm sorry to say I ain't packing lemonade or soda pop but try some of this Maryland Rye nerve medicine once I mix it with plenty of branch water for you. I heard Miss Judy was off duty last night and she still ain't back? I hope she ain't sick or anything."

Beth blushed but looked him in the eye as she replied, "She's indisposed. Does a lady have to say more than that to a man of the world?"

Longarm managed not to smile as he carried the fifth of rye to the wash stand to mix their highballs. He didn't know her well enough to remark that "indisposed" sure sounded more refined than "having the rag on." He was still mildly surprised she'd been that open with a mere man about a she-male tribal secret.

He handed Beth her highball and since she didn't seem tensed up about being alone in a hotel room with a man he tried sitting down beside her on the bed covers.

She clinked hotel tumblers with him, smiling as if sharing some joke. When she observed he mixed his drinks thinner than the folk back home on Prince Edward's Island he offered to fix her a stronger one. But as he was about to rise Beth put a dainty hand on his thigh to say, "Don't get up. This will do me fine, if you know what I mean."

He was commencing to suspect he knew what she meant. He sipped his own somewhat stronger highball, searching for a more delicate way to put it. Then, seeing there wasn't, he asked, "Are you sure you came here today just to tell me about those mysterious customers at the Harvey House?"

She calmly replied, "Well, I felt it my duty to tell a lawman about their suspicious behavior but, oh, Custis, if you had any inkling how tired a grown woman gets making silly young things behave when she knows exactly how they yearn to misbehave . . ."

So, seeing he'd heard about such inklings from other grown women, Longarm set his own tumbler aside, took hers to place on the bed table beside it, and the next thing they knew they were misbehaving fit to bust atop the covers with half their duds still on and from the way she was moving all she had to give a man he believed her when she sobbed she hadn't been getting any since Fred Harvey hired her to make certain nobody got any.

Chapter 19

Prince Edward Island, up Canada way, was still ruled by Queen Victoria. But you'd never know it, judging by the folk from up that way Longarm had met so far. He didn't think Beth wanted to hear about that Prince Edward gal who'd tried to do him the way Miss Delilah had done Mister Samson in the Good Book, bless her double joints. So he asked as they were sharing a smoke and some pillow talk if she'd ever met up with old Sandy McSween, the Prince Edward Island lawyer who'd married another redhead and started that Lincoln County War by charging the county machine head on, like some frisky range bull taking on a steam locomotive, with predictable results.

She pouted Prince Edward Island was way bigger than York State's more famous Long Island and allowed she hadn't known *all* the young range bulls back home. He decided Professor Darwin's evolution had been at work, with a limited number of Highland Rebels breeding themselves more rebellious as they married up with kith and kin. Her secret response to the Harvey gal's code of conduct was mighty rough on the bedsprings under them and when he laughed about that he couldn't tell her he was thinking about the time he and another gal had screwed clear through the bedsprings up Denver way that time and what a fuss his landlady had made over a little slap and tickle. He told he was just picturing the two of them finishing up on the floor. So that inspired her to take him on standing up against the wall and that was sort of rough on the wallpaper. Albeit most of the stains wiped off with a wet face rag and a dry towel whilst she sat on the bed, laughing like a sass writing dirty words on the blackboard.

So it was well after noon before Longarm ever got to read his morning paper and, seeing she didn't dare have dinner with him in public, Longarm went out to rustle yet another sort of picnic they enjoyed together in bed, once she had his duds off again.

What the love-starved Harvey employee demanded for dessert took a lot out of a man indeed, but he was up to going out for more beer and sandwiches when they next woke up.

Going at it dog style as the shadows began to lengthen some more, Beth confessed she wasn't used to living on sandwiches, either, and asked if they might risk ham and eggs in some secluded Mex joint she knew, come morning.

He waited until they were cuddled some more before he told her he had to get it on up to the Firehouse bright and early if he meant to be aboard a Friday morning combination to Fort Union.

Beth asked in an ominous tone, "Are you treating me to a one night stand? Who do you know in this Fort Union? Can she blow the French horn as loud as me?"

Longarm laughed and said, "I ain't about to ask her, even if she should turn out she-male! I'm headed for Fort Union to borrow a serious horse. All active service cavalry stock is faster than average. Officer's mounts can get faster than that. If I can, I mean to borrow sixteen hands or more of heavy duty riding off my fellow federal employees. After that, and this calls for some timetable study, I mean to get myself and said sudden horse up to Maxwell, where they'll be making up the Friday night-

Saturday morn milk train. I mean to be aboard her with a sudden horse and a serious saddlegun or more as she rolls for Trinidad. So then we'll see what we shall see!"

She said, "I'm getting hot again! If I'm only going to have this one night of love, you brute, I want you to fuck me bowlegged!"

So Longarm tried, and wound up walking a tad strange by the cold gray light of a Friday dawn as he toted his McClellan up to the station. After he checked it through to Valmore, New Mexico, and retraced his steps to the firehouse to see if Detective Caruso had checked in yet.

The burly Caruso had. He found a fifth of bourbon filed under B and they wet their whistles from time to time as Longarm brought Caruso up to date on the mystery men holding mystery meetings at the nearby Harvey House.

Caruso said he'd stake the restaurant out but asked what they might be able to charge any mysterious meeters with.

It was a good question. Longarm sipped thoughtfully before he decided, "Suspicion of mopery?"

"What's mopery?" asked Caruso, who added, "I've heard the term. I have heard of suspects being charged with it. But to tell the truth nobody has ever explained the charge of mopery to my satisfaction!"

Longarm nodded knowingly and said, "It's a hard charge to make stick because mopery ain't in the dictionary. But it sounds like something sort of suspicious and you can hold on suspicion alone as long as seventy-two hours and, what the hell, within the next seventy-two hours we ought to know what we suspect 'em of. I'm in the market for a heavy duty saddle gun. A Spencer .50, or better yet a .52, would be nice."

Detective Caruso replied, "We got all brands and breeds of confiscated weapons locked up in the property room. We may have some of those repeating cannon left over from the war. But don't hold me to that. Hardly anyone fires .52 caliber down this way since the South

162

Herd was shot off. Who are you aiming to blow such big holes through, Longarm?"

The taller and leaner lawman tersely replied, "I'm thinking the cover of mountain scenery. A .52 ought to plow through your average tree trunk and if it won't split a boulder it'll surely make the cuss on the far side *duck*!"

The portly local lawman led Longarm back through their second-story maze, scouted up a grizzled gray property clerk, and in no time at all Longarm found himself in possession of a Model 1865 Spencer Arms repeating .52-40, the gun that would have ended the war sooner if the Union Army had not been run by stubborn assholes.

Christopher M. Spencer had delivered his first seven-shot repeaters as early as 1862 and President Lincoln, after firing one on the White House grounds, had wanted to issue such a man-stopping whizz-bang to his whole army. But the political hacks of the vested interests had seen to fighting the whole war with inferior guns. Mostly the pokey muzzle-loading Springfield rifled musket.

As Longarm recalled all too well, those few troops on either side armed by mid-century standards, had cut through troops armed with muzzle loaders like hot knives cut through butter. Simply issuing men and boys single-shot but breech-loading Sharps rifles allowed them to get off way more rounds a minute, as Pickett's men learned to their sorrow at Gettysburg. Going up against the very few units armed with Spencer repeaters had been like putting a scared infant in the ring with a bare knuckles bruiser. At Chicamauga the Union Lightning Brigade and their Spencers had stopped Longstreet's Confederate Cream cold, and sent them running in panic from "That damn Yankee gun they load on Sunday and shoot all week!"

Longarm carried his time-worn but still wicked weapon back to the station in its own saddle boot. He lashed it just ahead of the saddlebags on the near side, opposite his faster sixteen-shot Winchester '73. Then he coffeed up in the Harvey House, not seeing anyone he'd screwed or wanted to arrest, before he boarded a southbound freight to get off at Valmora, around five miles from Fort Union, not too long after noon.

He hired a Mex with a buckboard to run him west to the cavalry post. He had to tell the whole blamed story at the officers club and stand a round when it came his turn. But in the end a troop captain who was proud of his horsemanship said he'd heard Longarm knew which end of the horse the apples fell from and agreed to lend his personal mount.

The critter in question was a chestnut Trakehner gelding, standing 17 hands in his matching black stockings. His name was Thunder. Longarm had no call to ask why. The big thundering Trakehner charger was the Austro-Hungarian basis for the McClellan saddle. When the heavy cav of the Austro-Hungarian Empire was ordered to charge it didn't whistle Dixie. It kept coming until you shot it to shit or it ran you down.

The young officer who loaned old Thunder to Longarm allowed he'd been looking forward to running over Apache at full gallop, but now the fool war department had that Colored 10th Cav chasing Victorio while he pulled garrison duty miles north of such action.

Longarm didn't ask if the captain had even heard a shot fired in anger. Sometimes you didn't have to and Longarm had been raised to be polite.

He let the friendly troopers treat him to a late mess, seeing it fit his timetable. Then he saddled and bridled the big chestnut, forked his ass aboard, and headed back to Valmora at a flat run, not to catch any train but to see how they'd get along at full gallop.

They got along fine. Old Thunder seemed to be just warming up to run serious by the time they made it back to town and Longarm had to haul hard on the reins to convince the big frisk they weren't really headed for the Atlantic Ocean that evening after all.

Treating Thunder to some carrots bought off a pushcart in Valmora, Longarm said, "You just run like so the next time I ask you to and we'll get along just fine, Pard."

Then a million years went by before they were able to board a northbound combination, get off at Maxwell, and wait more than a million years in a shitty little flag stop of say three hundred souls, most of them railroaders.

Since a good rider worries more about his mount's comforts than his own Longarm led Thunder to the only livery in town, explained his needs to their night man, and saw the big Trakehner got to wait in a dry stall with a bare back, no bit in his mouth and plenty of water and brouse to occupy him. He told the stable hand not to oat Thunder because they'd likely have to move some before dawn and it was a bother to run when you had to shit.

The stable hand, an older man with a missing left eye, said he'd noticed that during the war and asked, "Why do you reckon the generals always order the serving of a hearty breakfast the morning before the battle?"

Longarm shrugged and suggested, "Generals hardly ever get gut-shot full of ham and eggs and I suspect it eases a general's conscience to slap kids on the back and offer them treats whilst they order them to their deaths. I 'spose, like me, you learned to go easy on breakfast and fill up on coffee the morning of a big push?"

The other vet soberly replied, "Nice to meet up with another man who really saw the elephant. Half them soldiers blue out to the fort lie like rugs about all the action they've yet to see."

Longarm handed the older man a cheroot, lit it for him, and mosied on to the one saloon in town, mostly serving soldiers blue from the nearby fort. Longarm checked with a railroader he met up with and seeing he was way early, watched how fast and how much he put beer and pretzels away until at long last it came time to gather Thunder up and get on over to the sidings.

The milk train was already partly made up by the time it backed into Maxwell to pick up more cars, including the empty straw-floored car old Gilchrist had ordered them to provide for Deputy Custis Long and guest.

After he had Thunder up the loading ramp Longarm found their boxcar came with a sliding door in the middle of either side, with stanchions for riding stock forming a double row down what would have been the center aisle of a coach car. It could tear a mount's mouth bad to be held like a fish on a hook by the bit in its mouth as a rail car jerked back and forth under its hooves. So Longarm draped the reins loosely over the pommel of his saddle and slipped a rope hackamore over the leather bridle so's he could tether Thunder securely with a hackamore line to a stanchion on either side.

As the engine tooted up ahead Longarm was joined by one dismounted Colfax County deputy and two railroad dicks working for Gilchrist. They explained Colfax and Las Animas Counties were working together with the AT&SFRR that morning. A corporals guard of eight other riders were in the cars ahead. Four from each county. Other riders were posted every few miles *between* rather than *at* each milk stop. Longarm agreed that was pretty slick. The train jerked to life under them. Thunder seemed to know about rail travel. The railroad dicks took up positions covering either door with their ten-gauge Greeners. Then things got tedious as all get-out for a spell.

The first place they went was nowheres much, sitting on a siding to give Old MacDonald time to milk his moo-moo here and moo-moo there.

Nobody milked a cow before three A.M. After that they needed time to cart the milk to the nearest flag stop. So pick-ups started, from the south end, at four A.M. and proceeded north to stop every six or seven miles, taking around eight minutes betwixt stops to roll on into Trinidad before seven, Lord willing and they didn't get held up again.

They didn't get held up again. They made milk stop after milk stop until Longarm got to hoping somebody might suggest honey or vinegar for a change of pace. And then the morning sun was shining fit to bust and they rolled on into the Trinidad yards to unload behind Ruth Fenton's dairy a tad ahead of time.

Longarm wasn't the only one there, cussing, as he unloaded Thunder with a sincere apology and said, "We're going on down to this Mex livery I know, now. They'll treat you right whilst me and the other fool human beings figure out what we want to try next. I suspect it's over, whatever it was. They bailed their pal out before we could get him to talk. But they can't be certain we never got him to talk. So, right, they're long gone by now and I fear we'll never find out what their real game was!"

He rode far as the friendly Mex livery, dismounted, and introduced Thunder to the amiable old Mex, who declared him *muy caballo verdad*.

They were talking out front about the borrowed cavalry mount's care and feeding, pending further developments, when things commenced to develop a heap.

A young deputy Longarm had talked to earlier reined in his lathered paint to yell, "Thank God you told someone where you was headed! Mount up and follow me! All hell's busted loose up on Arizona Avenue in Nuevo Trinidad!"

Young Gordo, the skinny Mex stable hand, wailed, "Wait for me!" as Longarm and the Las Animas lawman were already riding off. Longarm had no trouble drawing abreast the other lawman's paint to demand, "What's up? What *happened* up north of the tracks, dammit!"

The kid yelled back, "They hit the payroll office of Las Animas Amalgamated with hundreds of mining men lined up for their hard-earned monthly wages! There were *five* of 'em this time, all dressed like cowhands as they rode *east* not *west* on those same fucking bays!"

Longarm said, "Shit!" and swung east at the corner of Main Street as he felt no call to ask where all the other lawmen in town might be just now. He knew most of them hadn't ridden back from their stakeouts along the rail line to the south, yet.

The kid galloped after Longarm through the morning traffic, bawling, "Where are we going? The robbery was up the other side of the tracks!"

Longarm yelled back, "I heard you. We ain't about to catch anybody at the scene of the crime. We're more apt to catch 'em where they're *headed* and you just said they were headed *east*, across open prairie, right?"

Chapter 20

The well-trained cavalry mount was sure-footed as well as fast. But bucking the early morning traffic at full gallop made more sense as you studied where the east of Main Street *led* a rider. Past the Posada de la Junta and a few Mex jacals beyond they were tear-assing along the old Santa Fe Train betwixt pig and poultry operations, in close, dairy farms further out, and then quarter-section homesteads on the rolling prairie farther east. The young deputy on the smaller paint kept calling for Longarm to wait up as he fell ever farther behind the rhythmic chest-nut rump and frisking black tail of the Trakehner charger. Then as if to add to his chagrin young Gordo overtook and passed him, riding a buckskin barb of no more than fourteen hands.

The secret lay in Gordo, riding bareback with a Henry rifle, added up to less weight for the buckskin to carry than a teen-aged gal. But after that Gordo wasn't about to catch up with Longarm aboard Thunder. He was barely able to keep them in sight, the way a fading marathon runner might cast wistful glances at the winner way out front and widening the gap. So by the time the three of them were far enough out of town to matter they were out of sight from one another save for dust on the horizon and thus neither Gordo nor the ever more lonesome county lawman could hope to ask Longarm what he, and they, were doing out this way.

Had they been able to converse at full gallop Longarm would have told them steeplechasing across a patchwork of fenced homesteads, dry washes and worse was way slower than galloping along the time-tested Santa Fe Trail, laid out to follow the best grades whilst avoiding hills, dales, or other obstacles betwixt whatever part of Trinidad they rode loose of and wherever they thought they were going. Most likely La Junta if they were making an honest run for the nearest railroad stop. All bets were off if they went to ground at some homestead, beef spread, or trail town along better than two hundred mostly wide open miles ahead. But the riders that would be coming along any time, now, would include locals who knew most everyone settled far and wide ahead, or feel mighty suspicious of any new faces this side of La Junta. So Longarm figured his best bet was to push on as far and fast as he and Thunder could, knowing they had to overtake even active service cavalry mounts across open range. He knew not even Thunder could make the better than two hundred miles to La Junta without let up. But if he didn't overtake them this side of the trail break at Tyrone he'd know they were hiding closer in and that would mean a whole new ball game. Billy Vail's process of eliminating called for crossing out the easy answers first.

As they topped a rise ten or twelve miles out of Trinidad Longarm saw a little old lady in a polka dot sunbonnet and mother hubbard doing a war dance in the middle of the dusty wagon trace, shaking her fists in the air like Indian rattles as she cussed a blue streak.

Longarm yelled, "Which way did they go?" as he galloped toward her. She yelled back, "Down the damned trail! Where else, the rude bastards? Rode through our barley lickety-split and laughing like Mexican jaybirds as they tore past! Who the hell are they and why were they cutting across our land from the northwest like so?"

Longarm reined in long enough to establish they were talking indeed about five riders on bays much the color as Thunder albeit not as rich and red a shade. She said she'd run out of her soddy, a furlong to the northwest, yelling at them to spare her damned barley in vain and she figured by now they had about a twenty minute lead on him. As he ticked his hat brim to thank her he saw Gordo on that chestnut coming over the horizon behind him. If the old lady was any judge of time the outlaws wouldn't be all that far over the horizon ahead. A fair horse could lope nine miles an hour or run flat-out at around twenty-five for no more than a mile or so. Figuring they'd be pacing themselves sensible he reckoned they'd make three or four miles in twenty minutes and you could see about that far when the prairie was rolling a tad less. So he heeled Thunder into full gallop whilst letting him set his own pace as he lived up to his name with his big pounding hooves.

The trail dipped some across a wide shallow swale. As they topped the rise beyond he spied an overloaded hay-wagon moving up the grade beyond laboriously, with its team of six leaning into their horsecollars as the she-male driver cracked her whip and cussed them in Spanish.

Longarm reined Thunder to a thoughtful trot as he recognized the not too tidy ragged-ass Mex gal driving in with yet another load of wild hay.

He reined to a stop and soberly sat his mount as she drove up to meet them. At easy conversational range he called out, *"Buentardes, Señorita. Tengo hambre. ¿Como encuento un cafetín?"*

She half stood behind the dashboard to point back down the grade with the whip, calling back in a convincing Border Mex accent, "They went that way! There are five of them! Have a care, *Caballero*!"

But that wasn't what Longarm had asked her. And any Spanish speaker who couldn't figure out as simple a message as, "I'm hungry. Where can I find a cafe?" didn't understand Spanish for shit.

So Longarm thanked her, if it was a her, and reined out of the way as if to let the bulky hay wagon pass as he shifted the reins to his right hand, casually drew the Spencer .52-40 from its boot on that side, and swapped rein hands again to open up at close range, blowing the fake Mex gal's black wig off with half his face and pumping seven rapid rounds into the loosely piled hay before he dropped the Spencer to land wherever it had a mind to whilst he drew and opened up with the sixteen-shot Winchester '72, while Thunder and those other army horses rolled their eyes but stayed steady, as they'd been trained to respond to gunfire.

By the time Longarm had emptied his magazine into the loose hay he'd been joined by young Gordo, who rode in yelling like an Indian and blazing away with his Henry. Then they'd both emptied either saddleguns and as Longarm drew his six-gun someone was yelling in a muffled way, "I give! I give! For Chrissake I *give* and please don't shoot me no more!"

Young Gordo asked, "Who have we been shooting at, *El Brazo Largo?*"

It was a good question. Longarm called out, "How many of you left and do you all surrender?"

The frightened voice called back, "Just me and Uncle Greg and he's hit bad! Did you get Baton Rouge, too?"

Longarm glanced at the Justin boots the figure in flamenco skirts had been wearing as he called back, "I reckon. Come out with your hands up and we'll talk about it!"

The unseen outlaw croaked, "I can't! I can't move anything below my middle and I surely hope I ain't spine-shot! Uncle Greg here took one in the chest and . . . Never mind, Uncle Greg ain't *with* us no more."

The Las Animas County deputy they'd left in their dust came loping on after them, calling out as he got within earshot, "What's going on! How come you stopped that hay wagon?"

Longarm let him get closer before he called back, "Appearances are deceptive. But now we know how they pulled that disappearing act over in the foothills. They'd drive this hay wagon up a box canyon or whatever behind two horses, with four left over for riding. Then they'd leave it, ride back to the tracks to razzle dazzle and simply gallop back to where they'd left less stock with this wagon. Once they had, they'd hitch the four with, say, two to make the usual heavy-hauling team. The one playing Mexican, half ass, would drive back the way they'd come disguised as a sort of ugly gal with his pals disguised as a load of hay. Let's unload some of this hay, now, and see what Gordo and me just did."

"This stable boy took part in the shoot-out?" marveled the Anglo lawman. Longarm replied, "Couldn't have done it without him. Betwixt us we emptied three magazines into all this hay and one of them still seems to be alive!"

They hadn't dug far by hand before they found a pitchfork behind the driver's seat and that speed things considerable. But by the time they had all four in the back uncovered, atop a quarter of the hay left, the spine-shot talkative Chuck Carter had bled to death. Four hundred and ten grains of spinning lead tore one hell of a hole in a man.

But he'd lasted long enough to introduce his pals. Uncle Greg Kellermann had only been hit in the chest by a two hundred-grain Winchester slug, as had the late Dutch Hart after an earlier Spencer round had crippled him for life, had he lived.

Baton Rouge Laval, the skirt- and wig-wearing driver who'd fancied himself a fair imitation of a Mex, had literally lost his head to Longarm's borrowed Spencer. By sheer bad luck Bobby Brandt had been hulled by a .52 and three .44s. Since Gordo's old Henry, the daddy of the Winchester, threw the same slugs, Longarm said he was

173

sure Gordo must have gotten that one. When the deputy questioned the ghastly exit wound left by the .52, Longarm said gut shots didn't do you in like much daintier holes in your chest.

Longarm had asked and Chuck Carter had allowed he didn't know any Toss Turner, adding Uncle Greg had once worked for Las Animas Amalgamated and hadn't confided every angle of his shell game to the owlhoot riders he'd recruited. When Longarm had asked the dying Carter where the money they'd just taken might be he got no answer. Chuck Carter had finished dying.

The hard cash wages of hundreds of coal miners drawing a dollar a shift for a month underground would fill more than a shoe box. But rummaging under the four of them with the pitchfork didn't produce anything. The county man allowed the outlaws had no-doubt cached their loot along the way. Longarm said, "It sure ain't in this hay wagon Why don't we haul it all back to town to sort things out? Gordo, would you care to drive that team if I tethered your pony to the tail gate?"

Gordo was more than willing. He had his skinny chest stuck out like a pouter pigeon's as he cracked the whip over and over, driving back through the Mex neighborhood on the outskirts of town.

Longarm, having reloaded both saddleguns but content with just the murdersome Spencer across his thighs, led the way with the county deputy guarding their rear. But nobody threw anything but kisses as they rolled along Main Street to be stopped at the corner at Maple and Main by a big sheriff's posse gathering to ride east at last.

Some town law, including Caruso, had possed up with the county men, as had the distinguished Farnsworth T. Binkle and a brace of company police working for Las Animas Amalgamated. It was old Binkle who recoiled at the sight of the bodies lined up in the hay to declare, "My God, that older one would be Greg Kellermann! He used to work for me! I never recognized him with that red bandanna over his face as they were holding us up!"

Another company dick explained, "Kellermann used to head up security. The boss, here, had to let him go for drinking on the job."

Longarm shrugged and said, "Seems obvious he wasn't on the payroll any more. Let's talk about that payroll. I've been adding in my head all the way back to town and they add up awkward. You surely know them better than me. So to save my pestering the bank, how many colliers might you have on your current payroll, Mister Binkle?"

The company manager replied without hesitation, "A little over twelve hundred, working 'round the clock in six-hundred-man shifts."

Longarm nodded and said, "So saying every collier averages a dollar a shift your monthly payroll had to top thirty-six thousand dollars?"

Binkle said, "Damned A and we want it *back*!"

Longarm smiled thinly and replied, "Let's study on where all that money might have wound up, then. The bank would have a tally on how much of it they delivered to you this morning as gold specie or silver dollars and smaller change, right?"

This time Binkle hesitated, but said, "We pay in silver dollars and don't confuse our immigrant help with smaller change. I know it sounds stupid but many a born American feels a stack of twenty silver dollars has a double eagle in gold beat by a mile."

As others in the crowd chuckled at the greenhorn notion, Longarm said, "I wish there was a nicer way to put this, Mister Binkle. But you are a fucking liar. There was never no robbery. You never brought no money from your office this morning. You meant to keep it all for yourself and your dead pals, here!"

It was the company dick to the right of Binkle who drew first. Longarm had figured he might, having seen that look in other desperate eyes.

So Longarm blew him out of his saddle with 410 grains

175

of spinning lead and most of the horses present, never having been gun-trained by the U.S. Remount Service sun-fished their riders every damned way. But the other company dick scrambled back to his feet in the swirling dusty confusion with his own six-gun out. Then the county deputy who'd been riding with Longarm dropped him with a round over the heart as he somehow managed to stay aboard his own gun-shy pony. That long run across open range had no doubt steadied it some.

Old Binkle as well as that undersheriff Longarm had been working with wound up side by side on their rumps in the same gutter. The somewhat younger undersheriff rose first to help Binkle to his own feet as he told him, not unkindly, "I fear you must be under arrest, Mister Binkle. Slapping leather on any paid-up lawman constitutes voluntary confession to this child and I can't wait to hear why Longarm just told you you were a fucking liar."

As he cuffed the company manager's hands behind his back he called out to Longarm for some explanation as to why he might be doing so.

Longarm said, "Thirty-six thousand silver dollars would weigh more than a ton. We were supposed to buy five jolly rogers scampering off at a run, each packing at least four hundred pounds of silver dollars?"

The undersheriff grinned up sheepishly to confess, "I never thought of that! I never considered an inside job!"

Longarm said, "They didn't want you to. That's how come they went to all that trouble establishing the notion of a wild and crazy gang of *out*siders working out of the Sangre de Cristos instead of our Mister Farnworth's office."

So the company man spat, "You're full of shit! I want my lawyer!"

Longarm replied in a more amiable tone, "You're going to need one. I'd be willing to put in a good word for you if you'd care to tell me why you had Toss Turner tossing bombs at me. To tell the truth, you had me as mixed up with that milk train shit as everyone else!"

Binkle didn't answer.

As others began to gather and steady the scattered ponies, Longarm suggested, "Why don't we just frog-march this clam over to the county jail and book him? He's facing twenty at hard in Canyon City, minimum, unless he'd like to turn states evidence against that killer still at large."

Chapter 21

Farnsworth T. Binkle never said another word before his lawyer showed up and the lawyer said not to say anything until he'd had a drink with the district attorney. So Longarm wired Billy Vail a progress report and that evening he got a wire from Denver ordering him to tidy up and come home. Billy said he'd already worked it out with Colorado politicos *he* drank with that Longarm's signed deposition would be enough to put Binkle away whether he turned states evidence or not.

The absentee owners of Las Animas Amalgamated already were, to the extent they could show on paper how Binkle and his fellow Dutchman Kellermann had not cut any other insiders in on their plot to rob the company blind.

Longarm had already returned that Spencer repeater to Firehouse Number One. He left Thunder in the care of that kindly old Mex and Corazon de Trinidad's new folk hero, Gordo Sanchez, whilst he enjoyed payday night with the boys in the back room until he wound up upstairs with the flashy-eyed court stenographer he'd had to spend so much time with, earlier.

Sunday morning he personally returned Thunder with a box of cigars and a commendation to Fort Union and after that celebration wound down he caught a northbound Denver & Rio Grande Pullman after wiring Denver his expected time of arrival, knowing Billy Vail wouldn't expect a hard-working deputy to report into the infernal office late on the Sabbath.

Sipping needled beer in the club car of a train that wasn't slowing down at milk stops felt way more comfortable than riding in a boxcar with even a nice horse. As he'd known when he waited an extra half hour for the D&RGRR, he didn't have to get off to transfer at Trinidad. So he didn't. And when a sort of interesting but sort of country brunette got on there to ride on up to Denver he decided to behave himself. Old Billy was such a fuss he might send somebody to meet the train and once back in Denver Longarm already knew plenty of brunettes and there were times just soaking up some well-deserved stagnation felt just swell.

As his train rolled north past Ludlow and the engine commenced to put its back into the effort Longarm was reminded, as he often was at such a time, of that forty-eight-hour pass in the biggest town a teenager off a West-by-God-Virginia farm had ever seen, and how downright giggle-wicked it had felt after hitting town with two months' pay and nobody fixing to order him about for two whole days, to have his filthy uniform drycleaned, check into the best hotel in town, and sleep alone around the clock, bare ass, betwixt clean sheets after a long hot soak in a genuine bath tub.

By the time his train rolled into Denver Longarm felt more than well rested and he'd just remembered he'd promised Freedom Ford an exclusive interview in depth once he got back. But first he had to get shed of his baggage. So when the train rolled to a hissing stop in Denver's Union Station he was on the steps with his heavily laden McClellan braced on one hip.

He dropped off frisky after all that unfamiliar rest to head down the platform for the exit closer to his southbound route on to his furnished digs on the unfashionable side of Cherry Creek.

He was swinging around an untended baggage cart with his own baggage when he was inspired to drop his load and dive head first over the cart by double-action pistol shots from close behind!

As he lay on his gut with his own six-gun out with the low platform of the four-wheeled cart betwixt him and whatever, a familiar voice rang out, "Are you all right, Pard?"

Longarm risked a peek to see Deputy Cohen from his own outfit just a few yards off, standing over somebody spread at his feet like a thick bear rug, and Cohen's six-gun was still out and still smoking.

Longarm got back to his own feet, gun still in hand, to move over and join them as he tersely observed, "Looks like I owe you, Abe. Billy send you?"

Abe Cohen said, "He did. Smiley's covering the far end. Boss said you were coming home with a killer left over and might need somebody watching your back. This him?"

Longarm made certain by rolling Toss Turner face up with his boot and replied, "It is. He tried to blow me up with dynamite, twice, down in Trinidad. What was he doing just now to inspire such rude behavior on your part, Abe?"

Cohen said, "Slapping leather. When I see a stranger grabbing earnest for his sidearm, and there's nothing to shoot at but the ass end of another lawman, I allow I am inclined to be rude about it."

Longarm hunkered down to pat the corpse down for evidence as he told his back-up, "He never returned for a sea chest full of dynamite he'd checked with the AT&SFRR. Still working on where he was going with it when he saw me as a target of opportunity. Must have noticed I was on my way back here aboard this train and boarded it up ahead where I never expected."

"Who was he working for?" asked the deputy who'd put a sudden end to Toss Turner's murderous plans, whatever they'd been.

Longarm rose, Turner's wallet in hand, as he replied, "Don't know. I thought he was in cahoots with that Binkle and Kellermann Billy must have told you all about. Makes no sense, now. How were they supposed to pay off with Kellermann dead and Binkle in jail?"

Cohen suggested, "Maybe they paid in advance?"

Longarm said, "That would call for honor amongst thieves indeed. Any member of the conspiracy to rob Las Animas Amalgamated who's still loose, and still within a thousand miles of this child, is by definition a damn fool. This son of a bitch was out to do me for somebody else entire. I wish crooks would stick to less complicated games."

Deputy Smiley, a tall morose Pawnee breed who had never smiled within human memory, came along the platform to declare, "I sent my pard to get the meat wagon. Nice shooting, Abe."

So that about ended it at Union Station that evening and by ten-thirty Longarm was granting that interview in depth to Freedom Ford of the *Denver Daily Commonwealth*, with a couple of pillows under her shapely but sort of compact hips. They did not, in point of fact, get into recent events down Trinidad way before he'd made her come, more than once, and they'd wound up propped up on more pillows against the head of her bed with her brown hair let down all over his bare shoulder and chest. Freedom was partial to pillows. Said a lady could never have too many pillows on hand in case she had company.

As they shared a smoke in the alltogether whilst holding thighs, Freedom pressed him for more details on those mysterious milk train robberies. She said she couldn't make any sense out of them.

Longarm explained, "Nobody was supposed to. The game they were playing was called Confusing the Issues.

They knew they'd have been suspected of just what they aimed to do if they just up and *did* it."

He took a drag on his smoke, passed it her, and explained, "The late Greg Kellermann had been allowed to resign under a cloud, letting his fellow Dutchman with a better crack at all that money keep his job after the board of directors had questioned earlier skullduggery. The sticky-fingered Binkle had been pocketing money sent to pay the colliers after docking pay for infractions Kellermann, as a lower-ranking security man, reported. Greenhorns speaking Greek or Italian didn't argue much over two bits here and two bits there, held back for not having a safety lamp screen in place or leaning a shovel against a tram that might be set to move any day now. We don't know for certain just how much they skimmed that way, or how many infractions were pure hot air. So far, the one we have still breathing to pay for their flim flams hasn't offered any help with the loose ends. But the owners' reconstruction works pretty good."

He had another drag for himself and continued, "Be that as it may. The two partners in crime knew their Shining Times were coming to an end. So with Kellermann already out of a job they decided to help themselves to a really big score. A whole month's payroll for a whole coal mine. After that they knew the owners would surely ask questions with earlier sneaky bookkeeping already under investigation."

Freedom snuggled closer to ask, "Wouldn't the owners have surely caught that sneaky Mister Binkle, once they'd studied his sneaky bookkeeping long enough?"

Longarm said, "That's why he wanted to clean out the till and make a discreet exit from the scene. He may have meant to resign in shame after letting those wild and crazy outlaws ride off with a ton of silver. The purpose of all that milk train nonsense was two-fold. It served as good *training* for the half-baked owlhoots Kellermann recruited for the main show whilst, as the same time, it had us all

182

convinced there had to be a gang of wild and woolly riders disconnected from any responsible adults in or about Trinidad."

She said, "Oh, I get it. Nobody was as apt to question Mister Binkle and the two company men working with him too closely about wild and crazy kids riding off with . . . a *ton* of silver, dear?"

Longarm said, "There were other holes in their scheme as soon as anyone looked close. That's how stage magic works. You're discouraged from looking close. But like the kid in the audience whose eyes keep straying to other parts of the stage, their whole act fell apart as soon as I got to wondering why I was looking at what I was looking at. I told you about an ugly gal driving a hay wagon at me behind six matching bays, more than the one time it fooled me. Finding no payroll money under the hay was all it took to remind me how heavy silver dollars were."

Freedom said to put out that fool cigar and let her show him how much she admired him for being so smart. But even as he did so she idly asked him, being a sharp reporter as well as a great lay, who they thought the late Toss Turner had been working for.

As he rolled into her welcoming love saddle Longarm said, "My boss, the terror of the paper trail, is working on that angle. We weren't able to get much out of old Turner, over to the morgue. Billy Vail's way better than me with dry facts and figures. He chided me for taking so long to weigh thirty-six thousand silver dollars in my head. Somebody laid out more than a thousand dollars, silver or otherwise, to bail Turner out of jail, knowing in advance he'd run for it. Both the lawyer and bondsman who worked that out have to know where all that money came from."

She was enough of a reporter, even moving her hips like so, to point out there was no way to make a retained lawyer or bail bondsman give away anything said in confidence by a client.

Longarm laughed indulgently and said, "No *legal* way, you mean. Don't let this get around, doll face, but old Billy drinks with Mom and Dad when us children have been put to bed with constitutional bedtime stories. So should Dad eat pussy or Mom take it in the ass now and again there's no call to shock us kiddies with the true facts of life, is there?"

That reminded her of this perversion she'd read about that she'd been waiting for an understanding bed partner to try and by the time the two of them agreed the notion was uncomfortable and overrated they'd clean forgot the late Toss Turner.

But Billy Vail hadn't and Longarm's faith in his paper trailing had not been misplaced. For while it was true nobody but officials of the Colorado Bar Association could convene a board of inquiry demanding some confidential but no-bullshit answers, the lowest bucket of slime practicing law in Colorado knew better than to bullshit them if he meant to go on practicing law in Colorado.

Western Union's records of wired money orders were played closer to the vest than the state secrets of the Czar of all the Russians. But where there was a will there were ways and an awesome amount of telegraph wire was strung across federal lands.

The bank the money had been drawn on was out of Billy Vail's reach and he didn't try, once he knew where Turner's pals had come by the money to wire his lawyer in Trinidad. Old Billy didn't need all the pieces to put the simple enough picture together.

So Tuesday afternoon, it having taken Vail most of Monday to work it all out tight, Billy paid a personal call on another gent he drank with now and again.

His name was Roberto Mendoza Garcia y Montalban but he liked his Anglo pals to call him Bob. His official connection with the Mexican government was that of a commercial rep, drumming up trade bewixt friendly

184

neighbors. He was never rude enough to repeat El Presidente's dry observation that Mexico was too far from God and too close to *El Pulpo Yanqui* as he tended to refer to the U.S. of A.

Once installed in the unfamilar position facing an imposing desk instead of behind it, Billy Vail lit the swell cigar the Mex diplomat produced and said, "It's none of my beeswax why a now-known-to-me bounty hunter and soldier of fortune calling himself Toss Turner, real name Thomas Thorpe, boarded a southbound train one of my deputies was on, with a sea chest full of dynamite."

The diplomat said, "I read about that in the *Rocky Mountain News*. If he was a soldier of fortune as you suggest he may have meant to peddle the dynamite to those border bandits you people keep on calling rebels, no?"

Vail said, "I ain't suggesting shit. I said that part was moot. Turner née Thorpe was a man on the make, looking out for himself. When he saw a chance to collect that handsome reward *your* side has posted on *El Brazo Largo* he changed sides. He wired your *Rurales* he was in position to kill a man they wanted dead or alive. They wired back to go on and just do him in, saying they'd take newspaper accounts of dead U.S. Deputies as proof Turner had his bounty coming. If you've been reading the papers as well, we're up to my senior deputy having Turner in jail and your government wiring money across the border to bail him out before we could get him to talk about all that noise on *our* side of the border!"

The smooth diplomat nodded easily and said, "I warned them not to do that. Would have been smarter for to leave that bounty hunter hanging out for to dry. But now he is no more, so . . . we are speaking off the record?"

Billy Vail replied, "We are and here's the deal. I've told the gent you call *El Brazo Largo* to go easy on them international incidents and he understands he's on his own

185

if he lets *Los Rurales* catch him *south* of the border. But the next time the cocksuckers you work for set out to assassinate one of my boys *north* of the border they'll never have to worry about rebels of their own breed again. Every damn one of my riders will be headed for Mexico City, armed and dangerous, with me leading them and to blue blazes with the Treaty of Guadalupe Hidalgo! I never wanted to call off that swell war we were having in the first place!"

So Good Old Bob allowed he was glad they saw things about the same way. Then the old hands shook on it and neither felt any call to wake any of the children up to explain how the world they were supposed to believe in really worked.

Watch for

LONGARM AND THE TALKING SPIRIT

305th novel in the exciting LONGARM series
from Jove

Coming in April!